Also by **Dennis Cooper**

The Marbled Swarm

A NOVEL

Dennis Cooper

HARPER ● PERENNIAL

NEW YORK ● LONDON ● TORONTO ● SYDNEY ● NEW DELHI ● AUCKLAND

HARPER PERENNIAL

HarperCollins books may be purchased for educational, business, or sales promotional use. For information please write: Special Markets Department, HarperCollins Publishers, 10 East 53rd Street, New York, NY 10022.

FIRST EDITION

Designed by Justin Dodd

Library of Congress Cataloging-in-Publication Data is available upon request.

ISBN 978-0-06-171563-1

11 12 13 14 15 OV/RRD 10 9 8 7 6 5 4 3 2 1

for Jesse Hudson

Chateau Étage, as a corroded iron plaque leads the unsuspecting to believe, lies a multi-hour car ride from my loft in the Marais and near a small town whose hyphenated name I keep forgetting.

The wooded property is vast enough to hold a hill of slight historical value and the makings of a river where the older son of the chateau's prior owner appears to have slipped, bashed his inebriated head against a rock, and drowned.

It was seeing this boy's picture and obituary in *Le Monde* that led me to case the home originally, and, according to a subtext, an alleged sighting of his ghost that caused his superstitious parents to put it on the market.

I asked a real estate agent who'd wielded acreage for my quote-unquote father to arrange a walk-through, more out of a morbid-seeming curiosity than any real interest in acquiring the location at that point.

I don't foresee a need to be explicit about the ping this death left in my irreparable imagination, as the consequences will speak out of turn and continually for themselves.

I'm at a loss to say why certain deaths strike me as secretive while others not so much. Granted, his full-fledged Emo look—which, if you were inattentive at the time, turned depressive youths into prêt-à-porter's backseat drivers for a season—left his hole in the world more romantic than most. Still, I suppose it could be argued that every new hole leads to anywhere else.

I will say for what it's worth that had he been singled out as a, oh, doer of good deeds, I might have sighed at his meaningless plot and turned the page.

Like every chateau I've had occasion to visit, mine appears to have been built exclusively to turn the heads and mist the eyes of peons driving to and fro along the corresponding road. Given the building's excessive age, no doubt its obscure architect had horse riders and peasants trudging on foot as his intended targets, but the bombastic effect has proven timeless.

I remember quite well how my tinier mind mistook the chateaux dotting France's far-flung hilltops for concise Disney castles when, in tragic fact, they're just giant farmhouses with a Napoleon complex. True to form, driving down my chateau's muddy driveway can cause one's car to seem a frilly carriage, but merely cracking the front door leaves you moping behind its magician's back.

Since my visit occurred on a weekend, the dead boy's father, Jean-Paul, mother, Claire, and younger brother, Serge, happened to be facets of the tour.

Jean-Paul found me suspicious until a bank statement closed the gap between my inheritance and the childish-looking features I control. I've learned to carry said documents almost everywhere I go, since I'm told my vibe suggests a cosmopolitan sixteen rather than the twenty-two-year-old worrywart I am.

Once the credentials were perused and returned, my politely nuanced interest in their loss combined with their addiction to all things him-related toppled a small bookcase's worth of gossip that would be tedium incarnate at this stage.

The family encouraged me to stroll, albeit supervised, about his former bedroom, a neat freak's cubicle containing nothing more of note than an antique desk whose drawers I lacked a good excuse to open and a short shelf full of DVDs and novels so anonymously trendy they're too out of print to even bother listing.

Jean-Paul singled out the wall where his son's paranormal image had been spotted distinctly if blurrily in the paint, and although I squinted, it remained a dead blank for the duration of my initial peek and show of concentration.

Before I imbed you in my story too repletely, let me single out Claire, the wife and mother, who might have suited my proclivity to look straight through almost any women I encounter had she not seemed more realistically a sister to young Serge, whose height she barely eclipsed.

This mismatch caused me to experience a most unsightly daydream in which a beet-red, hyperventilating infant gave birth to another crimson, screaming infant.

The aforementioned Serge, a childish-looking fourteen-year-old and hard-core Emo like his sibling, tastelessly offered to show me where the unfortunate's body had been found. I agreed before his parents could reprimand him, both for reasons that must be obvious by now and because, if I may be blunt, the boy was literally his brother's twin after a judicious edit.

Walking to the crime scene, I feigned admiration for how subtly his family or their gardeners had compromised their parcel of France's magnitude. They'd teased out a pleasant nature trail while wisely sparing their grounds the aesthetic lock and key that might have buried it in Frisbees and croquet sets.

While I bored my fellow hiker into an advantageous daydream, my eyes were busy with his more painstaking head of hair and outfit. With each footnote I ascribed to them, the more eerily he epitomized one of my "types," as those who shrink-wrap their opinions in set phrases like to put it. I have four, although, for the sake of brevity, I prefer to call them hot spots, each with its own set of qualifiers and subcategories, and they will queue up here later.

However, lest the term "type" mislead you, let me add that were I gay and not the creep to whom you'll turn the other cheek soon enough, I might have preferred, in Serge's case, someone tall enough that I could jab my tongue into his mouth without appearing unsightly.

Serge favored vintage black Slimane jeans, so tight in the legs that his near-robotic gait would have made Pinocchio a track star. His faux old-fashioned choice of a white and gauzy sweater flecked with Christmas trees was geared to mismate with a visible black T-shirt whose skull-emblazoned front seemed to represent his tortured soul's Peeping Tom. His limp, unimaginatively brown, forgotten-esque hair was worn in two chin-length, barely parted bangs that cordoned off a lightly made-up face so classic that, had he not been such a downer, it might have sucked fan mail into his in-box like atmosphere into a punctured jet.

So taken was I with the drab atmospherics and festive details of this crosshatched-seeming boy that I was caught quite off guard when his morose eyes rose just far enough to spot the bulge he had occasioned in my slacks.

I might have paused long enough to explain this billow was more undercover cop than confidant had his prying eyes not also signaled our arrival at the crime scene.

It was indeed a river wide and reliable enough to have inspired a crooked blue line on local maps, but not so pretty on the eyes or that much livelier than a cross-country puddle to have warranted a name.

To hear Serge, Claude had wandered off one night, drinking all the way, wound up here, and somehow suffered his unfortunate accident. He'd lain dead and undiscovered in the water so lengthily that when a groundskeeper found a bloated corpse, he mistook it for a heavyset trespasser in his fifties.

Even Jean-Paul and Claire hadn't recognized Claude in the gardener's wheelbarrow. They'd ordered the remains incinerated on a pyre, as had long been the custom in the region when discovering the hulk of an itinerant. But then Claude was discovered missing and not gallivanting elsewhere, and the unexplained and obvious were belatedly united with a plus sign.

Sharing this unpleasant detail seemed to weaken Serge, and he sat down heavily on the river's sloping grassy bank. When I asked him which slippery rock had done the damage, he grew even more forlorn and pointed vaguely at the boulder I had guessed.

As I peppered Serge with maudlin fanboy queries, his body slumped and trembled slightly under memory's weight. At the same time, his downcast eyes seemed increasingly taken with something about me, if that mixture of recalcitrance and focus is even possible.

The face I showed him in return could have led to every awful secret I possess, one of them involving him, but, using the hearsay that Emo equaled gay, or quite curious, at least, I wagered he was far more built to ferret sleaze from boys than their intentions.

On the off chance my manner hasn't made self-flattery a metaphoric gild to my veritable lily, allow me to infer that on the issue of attractiveness, I could spend many numbing if prettily over-written pages counting the ways in which my beauty is a fact, disputed by no one I've ever met, although I suspect a simple background check might do.

My father, or rather the man I will generally refer to as my father, cannot in truth take any credit for my layout. My mother, who was loosely an actress until my fetus trashed her waistline, appeared in a handful of films that the passage of time has revised from daring cinematic gestures to unwatchable displays of self-indulgence, usually playing a prostitute.

The last film in her middling CV was directed by the cultishly forgotten auteur and, more important as per my point, psychedelic heartthrob actor Pierre Clémenti, with whom, yes, my mother slept while on some drug binge, ultimately producing a child whose gradual enlargement would reveal to my father's glazing eyes a face that has struck more than one film buff of my acquaintance as scanned at high resolution from Clémenti's. Luckily, I have escaped his chalk complexion and, pray to God, his career-derailing hair loss.

Given the freedoms of that face, it's not difficult to flirt, or rather fake the act of flirting, when it's absolutely necessary, and so I did.

While Serge's signals weren't as gifted, or perhaps I mean well versed, unless winking and snorting has an erotic outreach to which I am immune, his new erection, plain as day and on the scrawny side, gave me the confidence to leer in his direction with ever greater effervescence.

"So, are you really going to buy this place," he asked.

I'm just rich enough to answer yes, I was, and even mean it. To be honest, I'd already concluded that the chateau's backyard, if one can tag a walled-off forest with that consolidating term, was a kind of Père Lachaise Jr. just waiting for any number of shovels to render its existence.

If that were true, Serge wondered aloud, could he store his drum set at the chateau, then practice after school and possibly on certain weekends? Their new home, he explained, was just a chip of tower block whose vaporous walls and floors would dash a career he'd embarked on at eleven.

While God is an idiotic premise, I often half wonder why it is that life, or mine at least, seems less to change from day to day than to be solved like an equation. For, not moments before, I had all but decided Serge would need to die before he suited me, and I had turned my attention to devising the first opportunity to see him crumpled on the ground.

Thus, I agreed to his request without so much as a torturing, in-between pause, and even added an uncalled for phrase regarding how nice it would be to spend more time with him.

While his head bobbed enthusiastically, and his somber eyes milked mine, I wiped the content from my face and suggested we return to the chateau, where I would state my serious intentions to his parents.

Retracing our steps down the trail that formed the property's chief thoroughfare, I began the lengthy process of discrediting Serge, as I call it, which you will come to understand is my modus operandi in these cases—namely, by plying him with questions about his likes and dislikes. Sure enough, and let me add that this assessment stood beyond his death, there was literally nothing worth archiving in the boy's head whatsoever.

It's true that until a year or two prior to that afternoon, I might have set myself the less ambitious goal of having some variety of sex with him, then, severely disappointed, as I've always been by sex, and worrying about the act's illegality, murdered him after a day or two or week of careful planning.

Had Serge been a sculpture, he would not have been a sculpture in the first place but a simple pedestal, although connoisseurs less rigid than myself might have argued that it held a cute if over-decorated bust.

By then we were approaching the chateau. I spied its owners chatting, cocktails in hand, as they awaited our return among the paths of a small, well-kempt garden. When the boy and I were visible amid the backyard's copse of centuries-old maple trees and flowery hedges, Jean-Paul and Claire waved, whereupon my young companion, flashing *v* for victory with both raised arms, trotted ahead to join them.

"Might I have a final look around," I yelled to those assembled, having waited to inquire until after the boy broke his good news, which I knew would leave the owners with no decision in the matter unless they wanted to be rude.

I left the trio toasting their new income and/or added storage space and made a roughly forty-minute study of the chateau I'd just hastily acquired.

In most respects, it was nothing but your average chateau, full of heirlooms only heirs would even bother to insure and elderly chairs and tables that only tourists could refer to as antiques. Where the walls weren't painted the rustic white of farm eggs, they were quashed by oldfangled wallpaper that did nothing but repeat a bleached-out scene of birds in flight at sunset.

The kitchen, with its chilly marble floor, tub-sized sinks, and the counter space to busy several chefs, did impress me since, as you'll come to understand, cooking from scratch, and by scratch I mean from autopsy to dishwasher, is far more than a spectator sport for me.

Still, what clinched the wisdom of my purchase was the basement, which I would later learn had been a penitentiary before the building formed its cap. It was still a simple, run-down jail, although its six small cells, each fitted with the classic metal bars and inclusive of an integrated swinging gate, held stacks of sagging cardboard boxes instead of gaunt prisoners.

Additionally, there was a metal door that locked a room that I would glean from doing research at the local city hall was once intended as a medical facility for the incarcerated, but had mostly been the site of unspeakable, as they always say, tortures and executions.

I'd just leant myself a decent budget to restore the basement's sullen antecedent when I spotted Serge's florid silhouette among the room's hazier shadows.

"Why," his voice asked, "did you say it would be nice to spend more time with me?"

Wait, have I mentioned that, prior to that afternoon, I'd committed several murders, or, rather, helped facilitate several boys' demises for reasons I'm withholding for the moment? If not, let me illustrate myself to that degree before I say another word, as it will shortcut this story to the expertise I'll now attribute to my curious behavior, and which I would otherwise need to bore myself as well as you with in the course of explaining.

As Serge fiddled with his bangs and grazed my calculating face, I rifled through my conquests, if that term is not too vibrant to apply to what amounted to fatalities, and settled on the tactics I'd used with reasonable success in an early and not so different case, although that boy was only twelve years old, and more important, my brother.

"Serge," I said, and cast an anxious look around, seeking to befriend his worries with my own, "what I meant to say back by the river was . . . You should think of the chateau as your home away from home, your getaway, your . . . tree house, if it pleases you. I could make up some official-sounding job to help legitimize this . . . well, peculiar-sounding, I'll admit, arrangement to your parents, when the truth is . . ."

I'd planned a lengthy, complicated answer interspersed with many thoughtful dot dot dots, but it seemed the boy had heard his password.

First positioning himself beneath one of the glary, dangling lightbulbs that crosscut the basement's abrasive-looking ceiling, Serge started rolling up his Christmas sweater's sleeves.

"Look," he said disconsolately, and, before I could, he gave those arms the job of similarly yanking up his skintight jeans legs, a task I could have told him was in vain, and which resulted only in the minor revelation that he wasn't wearing socks.

Still, in the time it had taken him to tug and fail, I'd scanned his arms sufficiently to get the gist of what I gathered was a "take it or leave it" type of offer.

Namely, Serge was, in the shorthand of that era's therapists, a cutter. When he was sad, which, judging from my initial scar count, appeared to have been often, he would hold a razor to his pasty limbs and slice into the flesh. Mostly, he'd left rows of unimaginative zigzags up and down his forearms. Occasionally, however, he'd gone bonkers and carved a word—I spotted "shit" and "kill"—or an occult-looking symbol, all for the purpose of . . . well, God knows.

In truth, I also know the whys as of this writing, but to tell you now would be to tinker unhelpfully with my story's glacial timeline.

Serge fished a razor blade from some compartment in his outfit and sent it fluttering in my direction, yelling words to the effect that I should find a way to use the blade to slash away his sweater, T-shirt, chest, and rib cage, and then reach inside and excavate his heart.

So, there he stood, or rather cowered, certain he'd re-pulsed me with his idiotic honesty about the blight awaiting anyone saintly enough to have given him the slight impres-sion that it would be interesting to fuck him.

Here's where I'll focus myself, or, rather, you can focus me, if you care, which you should, even those of you who see yourselves as reading from the cheap seats.

You're right to guess I half considered giving Serge's needi-ness priority, or, rather, right to guess my mind returned to times when, not yet knowing myself in the slightest, I'd done nothing but convince myself I was in love with one cute, sui-cidal basket case after another.

Truth is, my wealth is psychological as well as moneyed, and, in order to spare you some crushing verbiage, I'll ask you to witness my cruel-in-quotes decision for yourself and trust me when I say the bitch just simply had to die.

I told Serge quite succinctly that a death so premature would need evidence more damning than two nasty-looking arms, whereupon he literally snapped his fingers at the bright-ness of a dawning thought, then confessed to having mur-dered Claude.

His rambling, hit-or-miss admission was tellingly im-promptu, but I feigned a look of outrage, then furiously but carefully pried the offered razor blade from the floor's uneven stonework.

I held it to his throat, then, in a stroke of semi-genius that might warrant your applause were it not so self-serving, I caught his nerve-wracked eyes, then widened mine as if I'd just seen my own reflection there and found it damning.

My shaky hand released the blade and flopped onto his shoulder, then slipped and fell again onto the outcrop of his ass. In the guise of restive gayness, my fingertips were drafted in as spies, distinguishing the tight jeans's CGI from the more honest ass secreted in their shadow, bypassing the "ass" that owed its charm to being squished and repositioned to find the one that didn't deserve to be held hostage and strangled.

"Not yet," I said softly.

Serge was sent back to the garden, where I agreed to re-appear after an interval sustained enough to quell suspicion. Before he turned to leave, I withdrew my iPhone, initiated camera mode, and, declaring this a moment that demanded preservation, I captured him from every angle, including aerial.

By the time I joined the family in the garden, had my flute glass half filled with a slightly sour champagne grown and bottled in the region, and clinked their glasses' rims, I'd sent the photos to three . . . well, call them my associates for now.

Serge seemed . . . different—identical enough to be a twin but so sprightly as to seem fraternal. He was swigging bubbly and regaling us with gross-out jokes more suited to a child both half his age and a hundred times more outwardly conventional. In and of itself, the switcheroo might have had the vexing charm of a charade, were his eyes not wallowing in mine.

I quickly sent a text that hailed my driver from his bar or roadside, announced a prior appointment, and said I'd have my people draft a contract as required and send it to their people.

I offered them a warm, all-business hand. Claire seemed too tipsy to decipher it. Serge mouthed "call me later" and nearly squeezed it lifeless. Jean-Paul shooed the hand away with what seemed a secretive if kindly offer to escort me to my vehicle.

No sooner had a door banished the outdoors to a set of murals in the windows than Jean-Paul began to voice a most astonishing internal monologue.

To give you the framework, for it was lengthy, the "miraculous" return to form—or so he decreed it, complete with the quotation marks I've included—of "cheerful" Serge had not only been noted but enormously appreciated, as had my instigation.

"You'd never guess," he said, "but Serge was once the most overly excited and irritating child one could imagine. . . ."

It seems a meticulous hodgepodge of medications had made the boy marginally more tolerable, and the birthday present of a drum set had helped to siphon off a portion. But when his beloved brother, Claude, whose tastes and mannerisms he had mirrored and imitated almost since birth, was led astray into the dreaded Emo nonsense by an evil girlfriend, weak-willed Serge had naturally jumped the ship of reason along with him.

Suddenly, the mood swings that Jean-Paul had scrupulously tamped away became the truth, or so the boy proclaimed, and anyone hoping to drug him from his miseries was nothing better than a censor.

When Claude's corrupting girlfriend finally killed herself, that more pragmatic son had hung his spooky outfit in a closet like an American child on November 1. Serge, however, viewed Claude's return to baggy T-shirts and high-waisted jeans not as maturity in motion but as surrender. Thus, the only hero and positive influence who'd ever quelled Serge's Tesla coil–like infrastructure was displaced until . . . and here Jean-Paul's hand alighted on my shoulder, squeezing.

"Understand I'm just a dilettantish rich kid," I ventured, "but Serge's fondness for me, or rather its velocity, let's say, combined with the background information you've provided, leads me to risk causing you offense when I ask if, well, Claude might not have been molesting him, perhaps even consensually."

"There are those who find my son attractive," Jean-Paul replied after a moment's thought. "But I find them sorely lacking in appreciation for his enfeebled state, not to mention Claire's and mine."

"Perhaps they're more objective," I said carefully. "One could see a boy with issues, gauge the price and costs of getting laid at his expense, and decide, would one more mental problem make a difference?"

"Serge told us you've offered him a job," Jean-Paul said before exhaling in . . . discomfort, I would guess. "I'm tempted to include him in the price of the chateau, along with any furniture you'd like."

A chortle seemed to be in order, so I unleashed a tidy one. "If human trafficking were legal, I might say you've got a deal," I replied in a tone as dry as his.

"Trust me," he said, "my wife and I won't be alerting the authorities."

"It's not that I don't trust you," I responded. "Perhaps I'll pick my lawyer's brain about the current laws governing adoption. Even so, let's say I could accept him and, hypothetically, there came a day when my company's nourishment paled in light of suicide's problem-solving genius, and Serge just, well, up and . . . disappeared entirely? Any perks I might have gained from the arrangement would be used against me."

Jean-Paul's eyes were very busy with something or other in the room, but when I turned to appraise my competition, it was a wall no catchier than the quarter's other bulwarks, and perhaps even less so.

"If you have a minute," he said, "I'd like to show you something else about our . . . excuse me, your chateau. You seemed to feel at home in Claude's room. Why not enjoy it at your leisure, and I'll go separate my wife and Serge, then join you."

After a refresher course vis-à-vis the room's location, I headed up the central staircase, pausing every other step to view one of the family's photographic portraits, which decorated my ascent in a diagonal, salon-style row.

All but one of the portraits seemed to predate Serge's Emo phase, and, to make what I'll admit is an offhand judgment, I understood Jean-Paul's unease at the reemergence of that crazy-looking, boisterous child.

He seemed a mugging headache of a creature, each twisted face and flipped bird more intolerable than the next. That said, never having faced his line of fire, my daydreams were allowed to be indecent, and I was struck, to use my own term—if no doubt quote-unquote "turned on" in yours—by . . . aspects of the boy—genetic offshoots or what have you—that perhaps—and even that "perhaps" is offered lightly—might only have impressed the coach at his *ecole* or pleased their family pediatrician.

I found Claude's room casually enough, and, seeing nothing new, withdrew every drawer from the antique desk, laying them side by side upon the bed and rifling through their messy contents.

It took several layers of old homework, birthday cards, and ticket stubs for disappointing concerts before the smallest of the drawers produced something inexplicable in the form of five or six unopened envelopes addressed simply to The Liar.

I tore one's edge and winnowed out its letter. Although unsigned, the seismic script appeared to finger Serge's hand, and while the writing blackened into folk art every time it promised to get juicy, the author's point was unmistakable.

I have a tendency to overanalyze, which must be backpage news by now. On the plus side, you've witnessed how this helped me parry with Jean-Paul, but, more often than not, I deal with boys, and usually screaming, pleading ones at that. Hence, I can waste untold quarter hours seeking inference within inference where none exists at all.

Rather than transcribe my wordy thinking, let me scrape into the future while presaging this foreshortened moment with the caveat that, in time, the letter in question would lend itself multiple interpretations before its meaning disintegrated entirely, like when human bones are dunked in vats of acid.

I heard the sound of carpet being crushed and deftly stuffed the envelopes into my pocket, expecting to turn my angelic smile upon Jean-Paul. Instead, it was a woozy, slurring

Serge who nearly tripped into the bedroom, did a pratfall on the bed, and restarted our one-sided handshake in the garden, but with my crotch as the recipient.

Were I even half as gay as you imagine, I might have rearranged my schedule for the next few days and fucked Serge until his epidermal layer collapsed around his neck like an old white sock. Not that I'll claim such a scenario is utterly beyond me, at least as an exploratory prologue, and . . . fine, I'll go ahead and say what I've been hesitant to spill for fear you'll simplify me prematurely.

Truth is, Serge's body, albeit mostly guesswork and packaging-related magic at that stage, had been gnawing—well, to be more honest, being gnawed at in absentia—long before my hunches were corroborated by a certain family photo of Serge et al. reclining on the beach, which I only didn't mention when I was standing on the stairs because erections make me fumbly.

I'll accept that gnawing's impact on the horrors he had coming just so long as, in return, you get the thought that I'm some average child molester out of your conjectures right now. I promise if you grant me that inch, you'll feel roundly less embarrassed a dozen pages from now.

For all their sloppiness, Serge's fingers could have been a master potter's and my crotch their spinning wheel. In fact, I might have clipped two of his fingers to my zipper had I not noticed a strange, grinding metallic sound I didn't recognize offhand.

A bedroom wall was in the process of discoloring. Given the gray and stormy cast of the newer marking, I initially mistook it for a shadow, perhaps one cast by us. Then it grew, quickly engulfing the very wall where Jean-Paul claimed to have seen Claude's ghost, whereupon it seemed less a shadow than a mirror that reflected not the room but some malingering counterpart.

I stilled Serge's busy hand, then roughly turned his head until our viewpoints were in line. By then the wall's effects had, well, perhaps "coagulated" is the term, into an image that so obviously depicted Claude in his classic Emo era, even a relative bystander like myself would have sworn to it on camera.

He was floating, I suppose, since his misty-looking Keds pedaled air several centimeters from the floor. He approached us in theory, yet seemed as wedded to the wall as any movie to its screen, so, in a sense, he was marching harmlessly in place, but with the troubling determination of a "walking" mime.

I'd never seen a ghost, nor thought death gives its inmates visitation rights. Still, I'd watched my share of so-called paranormal sighting clips on YouTube when bored enough, and, I'm sorry, but I'd never seen a ghost show up anywhere, no matter how opulent the haunted house, in full color and in high-definition like this supposed Claude.

"If he'd looked like that when I killed him, I wouldn't have done it," Serge slurred. "I wonder what it means."

Suddenly, as though incensed or bored by Serge's quibbling, the apparition, well, less dematerialized, as one expects of thinning fog, than switched off, lamp-like, accompanied by the same muffled, grinding noise I'd heard earlier.

Now, a hefty chunk of wall rattled free of its foundations. Reborn as a crude door, it swung open to expose a large and very bare-boned closet, although the vestibule seemed less a niche set aside for worldly extras than a kind of world unto its own, no more servile to the bedroom than an attic is a secondary ceiling.

Standing in the heart of this compartment, partly obscured by viscid dust, whose fog-like whirling briefly lent him the aura of, say, the aging Johnny Hallyday in concert, was a disheveled Jean-Paul, his eyes glaring at his audience of two.

"Is that true, Serge?" he asked evenly, the kind of evenness that would allow brain surgeons to win every steady hands contest if such a prize existed.

By then, my eyes had grown conditioned to the weakened light inside the inlet, or at least enough to parse a strange black lump of shadow on the floor as an old Sanyo projection TV circa the early '90s. I might have thought its silhouette was Jean-Paul's robotic Egor were I three years old and had I not grown up watching a television of its very make and model.

In that second, the so-called ghost was debunked, its molecules re-boxed, and its perpetrator busted.

I was so preoccupied that, by the time I felt the mattress roil and quake beneath me, it was an aftershock. Serge had disappeared, leaving only an anemic stink of champagne crossed with whiffs of hair gel, and most likely a commotion that was happening down the hall.

Jean-Paul looked strangely nonplussed for a man who'd turned a boring wall into a channel, much less a father who'd just seen an alleged killer in his own child's face.

I hardly knew which newfound thing to question first, but while the vestiges of Serge's fingering nearly dug my hand into the pocket full of letters, then fanned them like a winning hand of cards, erotica, as should be clear by now, cannot compete for my affections with an interest in subverting its effect.

Allow me to edit Jean-Paul's press conference to smithereens because, while its gist does need to fortify your intake, this story will be headier if it leapfrogs this peculiar episode. Plus, I need to start herding this section back to Paris.

As for Serge's guilty plea regarding Claude's death, Jean-Paul pronounced it destitute. The corpse's single injury had been a gash in the head's corroded crown. Thus, Serge, whose height failed his older brother's by at least half a meter, would have had to lie in wait with a ladder or have perched amid the treetops with a slingshot, and his restrictive jeans alone would have prevented that.

As for the ghost trick, it was artless enough. To function as a door, the mobile portion of the wall had been hollowed out—its consistency akin to stretched and painted canvas. Thus, any image projected at its homely, somewhat porous underside seeped into the bedroom and degraded mystically enough.

As for why the ruse was called for, it seems Jean-Paul had wildly overdrawn the family's bank account for reasons he left blank. The chateau's value formed the only refill, but Claire would never have agreed to sell without discovering his debt, a bombshell he said he simply couldn't chance.

Fortunately, Claire blamed ghosts for every misplaced car key, so he'd put that quirk and their tragedy together, asked their hysterical housekeeper to clean Claude's room, switched on the projector, then run to investigate her screaming and yelled his head off too.

Once Claire was scared into a mumbling insomniac for several days, Jean-Paul had casually reminded her that Claude's last known words were, "Die, you fucking bitch," whereupon the chateau was on the market within a week.

As for the threshold he was standing in, he described it as the lobby of a secret labyrinth, and he invited me inside after a warning that, while I would safely reemerge, my outfit mightn't, whereupon I crossed the room and stood uncomfortably close as he shut the groaning door behind us.

Essentially, we were packed inside a wooden box, the sort of grand yet chaste container that must have carted *Venus de Milo* to the Louvre. In one direction, a second doorway had been sawed with minimal efficiency, and, through it I could see a hallway sculpted from the space between the chateau's widely separated walls.

To negotiate this narrow thoroughfare, we had to jerk our bodies sideways, duck beneath its low-slung grater of a ceiling, then scoot along in little increments, scraping dust from everywhere until we'd inched into another roomy crate.

Jean-Paul's fingers traced one wall until they felt a pierce or tiny gap. Once this gouge was capped off with an eye, it became a peephole, round yet not quite circular, like a prostitute's asshole, that allowed one to spy on a surprising portion of the chateau's master bedroom and, in my eye's case, an inhabitant as well, specifically the half-undressed and napping Claire.

Had my faculties been less congested, I might have seen or thought I'd seen an unknown actor who'd been playing her up to that point. Her long blond locks were flowing down a head-shaped clump of Styrofoam, and the short-haired, topless body snoring on the bed had everything a teenaged boy could use.

My surprise was such that, as Jean-Paul and I began to venture farther through the maze, I risked a quip about his wife's androgyny, which he brushed off as a common side effect inside the tunnels, perhaps resulting from a gas leak, whereby the non-secret world could start to look too vivid.

Another passageway, as crimping as the first but L-shaped and wrapped around a chimney, snuck us to a third, slightly more livable compartment. In truth, were the trek and puzzle to locate it not so testing, I might have guessed a homeless man had set up shop there.

A metal high stool accessorized this alcove's peephole. To its right, a plastic garbage can was filled with crumpled papers, each ball graffitied by a hasty, scribbled text. While it's possible this can's unpleasant stench came from the gas leak Jean-Paul mentioned, it reeked of sperm.

Sitting on the stool, I peeked into a room that, while not formally introduced as such, was, between the hogging drum set and an unmade, bloodstained bed, not exactly crying out for Serge's passport.

If I had hoped to spot a gun left smoking by our chatter in the basement, and I can't say that was precisely my intention, the only quirk lay in a checkerboard of posters that occupied one wall. Owing to the angle, I first mistook one poster's subject for an image of myself, then, as my paranoia eased away, for a dated souvenir from Pierre Clémenti's youngest days, until I finally realized the boy was Claude, his hair longish but not yet codified by Emo.

When I returned my eyesight to the secret vestibule, Jean-Paul was waiting in a corner where, gulping at his feet, a more or less square hole had been sawed out of the floorboards and framed with a fluorescent strip of tape long since too crispy and burnt out to be of help.

We stepped inside, Jean-Paul first at my insistence, whereupon a simple ladder dropped us to the ground floor. There, another secret chamber, this one lofty and more mindful of a chapel than a carton, formed the anchor for another set of passages and rooms, whose hidden door and peephole combinations menaced the living room, Jean-Paul's study, and the kitchen respectively.

Jean-Paul snatched a flashlight from some inlet and, after clicking to ascertain it was workable, we descended through another pitch-black square, where the ancient-smelling air signaled we were fully underground.

The room in which our feet touched down, the seventh by my count, looked to be a naturally occurring cavern prearranged by craggy rounded walls and an uneven hard dirt floor.

In one direction, the cavern seemed to dilate into a cave, and while Jean-Paul claimed it was no deeper than your average bathroom, he declined to tilt his flashlight and reassure me.

Directly opposite this so-called dent was a final exit that, when pushed, transformed one of the basement's grungy jail cells into a turnstile, which, despite its girth and weight, spun as lightly on its axis as the revolving doors at Galeries Lafayette.

To say I felt amazed by what I'd seen would be forcing things a little. "Amazed" is not the problematic word, but rather the idea that what had been uncovered was miraculous. For while my awe, which coalesced within a privacy where you remain unwelcome, was not inconsequential, it emanated from a very strange coincidence.

You see, the home in which I'd spent the greatest portion of my life also hid a scrawny, ill-lit secret realm similarly fashioned from the hollows of the normal-looking house, and, while far less of an involving place than the chateau's, I assure you it was just as wicked.

I tidied up my outfit, plucking splinters from my coat sleeves and slapping dust out of my trousers, while Jean-Paul, now quite agitated with excitement from having made a confidant, began telling me the secret tunnels' curious history.

To hear him, they'd lain dormant in the chateau's walls for many years. But one night, amid a burst of curiosity about his fellow townsfolk, whom he had long dismissed on sight as Jean-Marie Le Pen fans, he'd ventured to a popular café and ordered several drinks.

Most of the patrons certified his base suspicions, but one

man, whose outsized taste for cocktails seemed to make him something of an outcast, had introduced himself and asked Jean-Paul if the scuttlebutt was true that he was living in the chateau known to locals as the weird one.

Several Kir Royales later, the woozy gentleman confided that the chateau's prior inhabitant had offered him a tour in return for oral sex when he was younger, a tit for tat he'd only agreed to since he was reading and enjoying a novel by Jean Genet at the time.

The secret passages this gentleman described were, first of all, too infinite and city-like to hide within the chateau's modest structure, and, second, had been faded by his years of heavy drinking, leaving lots of creepy talk but not the vaguest hint of how this alleged kingdom might be entered.

It had taken a wary but bewitched Jean-Paul several months to find a strangely fulsome wall crack, then, using the old credit card trick popular with movie burglars, swipe an unassuming kitchen cabinet into a creaking, abstruse entrance.

It was then my iPhone pinged, and I excused myself, taking several steps into the basement. When I saw my driver's number, I nearly slipped the phone into my pocket, but, perhaps hoping to enjoy a few more seconds to myself, I dutifully clicked "Read."

"Some boy . . ." his text began, had asked to hide out in my car and return with us to Paris—a bad idea, he thought, but one the boy claimed had my preapproval.

Based on what you've read thus far, you must think Pavlov's dog could have texted him my answer. While your assumption is correct, I'll instruct you once again that jumping to nefarious conclusions won't flatter you much longer.

For the record, I authenticated Serge's lies and suggested that my driver fold him up inside the trunk.

I would have offered Jean-Paul my hand in parting had he not seen it coming and insisted that, before it clasped his, we share a single drink upstairs and dot the *i* on one or two outstanding matters, as he put it.

After using the official staircase as a shortcut, Jean-Paul ducked into the chateau's pantry and retrieved an uncorked Sauternes and two glasses before leading me outside and onto what I believe is called a veranda.

It held a single café table and two painted, sun-grilled metal chairs that would have roasted us, but, before I could suggest a walk instead, Jean-Paul dragged the ensemble beneath an ivy-strewn overhang.

First we sipped, gazing at the acreage that was just a signature away from being infamously mine. I weighed a grassy alcove between two gingko trees and then a flower bed boxed inside a waist-high hedge as likely candidates for Serge's grave site, while a grim and staring Jean-Paul seemed to mourn the property itself.

"The truth is . . ." he said. "It was I who murdered Claude."

His eyes were swooping in accordance with a vast flock of birds that circled high over the backyard at that very moment for its own and fractured reasons.

"Some months ago," he continued, "Serge confessed or lied to me that Claude had been raping him for years. The shock was . . . well, calling it a shock will surely do. You can't imagine how profoundly these alleged, covert acts attracted me since I have no ideas in that regard myself.

"Serge is gay, you must agree, and you . . . well, you're whatever style of predator you are, but my perversions don't explain it. No, there was something else. I knew Serge was fabricating, or I knew he had to be. I would have seen them through the peepholes, and, if I'd seen them, I would have called in the police like any father.

"I've watched my sons masturbate a hundred times, and those flares of unseen skin and stiffened penises never engineered even the least tingling of sensations. No, it was the idea, the concept, the product of Claude sodomizing Serge I was obsessed with. It seemed so cataclysmic next to what I had been seeing.

"I told my family I was writing a novel—a strange premise, perhaps, but I had written one when younger, imitative of Robbe-Grillet and unpublished, of course. Thus, I would be locked inside my study for lengthy periods of time. Instead, I wandered in the chateau's secret passages for months on end, hoping to get lucky.

"I did in fact write and quite voraciously, as you might have gathered from the overflowing trash can in the small observatory next to Serge's room, but, in that unusual case, words proved to be a mere emasculation of reality.

"When Claude and Serge did nothing more vituperative throughout those months than stare each other down, I decided to kill them both. The reason for that is very complicated.

"I eased through Serge's secret door one night and suffocated him with a pillow. I'm certain he was dead because . . . well, in the confusion of my feelings, I sodomized his cadaver with a violence that would have coaxed a pterodactyl from its fossil, be assured. But, to a horror I was scarcely able to conceal, he came downstairs for breakfast in the morning with nothing more unpleasant than a headache.

"For a time, we had a gardener whose relentless gifts to Serge, even on the most infinitesimal of holidays, must have worn away his salary. I invited him to share a beer at this very table, and, after a bit of yard talk, let's call it, I suggested he could tamper with my son so long as Serge died inexplicably while on their date and by some odd coincidence.

"I unforgivably neglected to insist the encounter must transpire in Serge's bedroom. I felt so stupid. They did their business in the tool shed, and, to worsen matters, Serge was such a "hottie," by this gardener's estimate, that accidentally killing him would be impractical. I fired this gardener, and he blackmailed me. He's still blackmailing me.

"One night, an inebriated Claude mistook our backyard for a pretty park. I followed him until I knew our yells would fray against the chateau's windows, then grabbed a rock and, waving it in upraised hands, confronted him. Had he raped Serge? I bellowed. 'Only in the mouth, and once, and he raped me if anything, and hardly even, but you . . . Serge told me you've been raping him for years. So, cut the motherfucking—'

"This charge so aggrieved my mind that it seems I used the rock to answer him. The head blow didn't kill Claude, but it left the things he tried to say incomprehensible, and his legs could not support his weight or even crawl. I dragged his slurring, flapping body to the river and laid it facedown in the water. And, to be fair, I somehow viewed myself as an avenging angel and raped him as well.

"Strangely, Claire thought Claude was partying in Paris, and Serge and he weren't speaking, and we were in between groundskeepers at the time, so when someone finally breached that distant part of the estate, Claude's body was so waterlogged and bloated, it might as well have been Amelia Earhart's plane.

"Obviously, Serge had to die for, well, there are millions of compelling reasons, trust me. He had an expiration date, but, between the game of selling the chateau and hosting buyers day and night, coordinating the two schedules has proven difficult. So, are you going to kill him, or what are you going to do with him?"

The flock of birds had spiraled elsewhere, and Jean-Paul was gazing at the empty sky, which had nothing left to hint about itself unless blue air knows something I don't know. Naturally, I'd been balancing my intake of his words with their presumptive trust and strangely smooth delivery.

I don't believe in honesty, or not in fecklessness so thorough as to wipe a liar clean. There's a reason why the recent drip-drip-drip of missing French boys has made the headlines without a single gendarme, worried parent, or gutter journalist showing signs of having given me a thought.

Granted, when people disappear in bulk and every one inspires a Facebook tribute page whose friends are under twenty-one and gay or female—and not to staunch this story's flow to compliment my tastes, but the unsolved spree has not been tagged *"la reconstitution historique de beauté mauvaise"* for no good reason—their abductors rarely beg for chloroform as well. So, there's that distraction to assist me.

Tweaking every word before it moved my lips, I told Jean-Paul that, circumstances being what they were—and I roughed out certain issues we'd discussed, then divulged Serge's location—a bit of news that didn't seem to faze him in the slightest, I'll add—I couldn't see the boy living more than, say, a day or two perhaps.

"This is terrible," Jean-Paul said, "but . . . would it be possible to . . . observe the ending? While safely hidden in the passageways, of course."

I replied that were his hands to wind up dirty—the form of dirt to be determined—which would likely need his DNA and necessitate his posing for some grisly family portraits, all of which would stay locked in my possession if uncalled for, and were the chateau's secret walkways reenvisioned as a hiking trail that wended up a man-made mountain, I could promise any highlights would transpire within its scenic viewing spots and most conceivably, as strange as it might sound, in the kitchen.

Jean-Paul forced his jittering, inattentive eyes into a collision with mine, or at best I seemed to be their second choice.

"If I appear distracted or withholding," he said, "it's because this property has a deeper and more thorough secret, concealed from you until this moment, and in light of which even the passages I showed you will seem as public as a sidewalk. In truth, the chateau is a kind of theater, and its rooms and floors and private berths a tiered and complicated stage where my family and I form an involuntary cast. Never having cause to give it words before, I can't think of how to phrase this."

I have a tendency to blather when a thoughtful "hm" would serve, and yet so taxing were my feelings of confusion and disinterest that I smiled suspiciously, then shook my head to show I hadn't understood a word he'd said and likely never would.

He seemed perplexed by my misgivings, although, as years have passed and superseded his inflationary image of the chateau with my own, I've revised his cringe and worried gaze across the yard into a look of disappointment.

"On second thought," he said, "it will prove more understandable if you discover it yourself."

My car is a customized Citroën Hypnos, and I don't believe you need to know much more about it other than, perhaps, a hasty rundown on the actual revision.

The backseat was enlarged and gussied up in hopes of holding and impressing up to five short, skinny guests—six, if one or two of them have died, by which I mean are put to better use as unwitting contortionists.

This reshuffle chopped the trunk into a wedge unsuitable for luggage and barely large enough to cram a corpse, much less a boy with working lungs who also has a multilayered Emo outfit and detailed hairstyle to consider.

No sooner was the driveway's crust of twigs and pebbles crackling beneath our tires than I heard Serge's . . . fist, I think, bang repeatedly on something. Due to his lack of elbow room, the sound was pleasantly non-bell-like.

Azmir, my driver, has lived in France since he was ten, thanks to an epicure of scale-model Algerians. When his appointed week or two of lopsided sexual recipience were up, a gory head wound would have exiled him in Jannah had he not overheard his owner ragging on a newer harem dweller and taken it upon himself to kill the little loser on the spot, apparently so charming his master with this burst of loyalty that he was spared and given tenure.

Years later, my late father hired him as a driver and, rather oddly, fattened up some bigwig's bank account to make the boy a citizen. Thus, Azmir's sleaze factor and flying off the handle are so ingrained within my worries that to this day I can't sit behind him without fingering my mace.

Azmir's choppy voice is far too brazen for my fussing speech to illustrate, so I will neither butcher nor adorn it, except to share that the sentiment behind his first few words was "I need to fuck the weirdo."

It seems a manageable demand, and I'm scarcely a monogamist. Still, to use a lingo I revile and yet can wield if called upon, Azmir is hung like a fire truck. While that aphorism works, its charming "fire truck" grossly underplays the threat.

So, before you find his macho, well-armed act endearing, let me add that while he'll fuck whoever I request until they're floating like a raft on their escaping blood supply, that indiscrimination is in his job description.

What Azmir craves are ten- to fourteen-year-old white boys, or, to be precise and yet more general, their pale, outnumbered asses, or, to bring in a microscope, making Serge's, for example, seesaw, blow gaskets, suffer quakes and aftershocks, and finally flatten like a leaky tire beneath his Herculean pumping.

Honestly, I would have paid him overtime and even held our captive down until the corpse had shit an octopus of its internal organs, but there are others in my posse, each a shade of gay, or so I'll lazily baptize them for the moment, whose preference for working ass is moot whenever Azmir gets carte blanche, and I was pretty sure that one or two held IOUs from me.

So, I told Azmir I'd have to put his need on hold, which he knew I would say and surely hated.

It was our stony, ensuing lull that brought the graduated pace of Serge's pounding to the foreground. The beat was slowing, in a word, and I might have blamed his spindly, tiring arm if each new tap-tap hadn't sounded more insistent than the last.

To be safe, I cracked the backseat's secret hatch, as I call it, although it's technically the car trunk's skylight. As Azmir hadn't charged the car's official flashlight as I had asked, I tried to figure out the trunk by squinting, and when that proved no match, I used my nostrils.

Cuteness is significant, no question there, but in my . . . field, as I'll describe my predilection for the moment, a boy's outlay is always something of a cheesecloth. In Serge's case, I smelled a recent cigarette, unlaundered feet or socks, mouthfuls of breath bequeathed by pizza, and what had to be a hard-on, and not an instant one at that.

Serge must have felt a draft because his noises ceased, and he said, "Please don't become angry with me, but I can't seem to breathe."

I asked if doing "this" was an improvement, and then I raised and dropped the hatch to illustrate my "this."

"Too early to tell," he said.

I asked if he would pique my curiosity and say whether or not he was sporting an erection.

"Yes, but any credit goes to how I'm stuck here and the shaking of your car," he said with difficulty.

I gave him the good news that we were looking for a dirt road where his seat could be upgraded, and then the bad news that the dirt would make the ride conspicuously bumpier.

"If it's no trouble, can you leave it open," he asked, meaning the hatch, which I immediately closed.

Northeastern France is very harmless with its hills in quotes, repeating fields, and sprinkled trees, and quite serene thanks to its last-ditch status among tourists, but it persecutes me nonetheless for reasons I can only play at solving.

One of my family's vacation homes lay somewhere in this region, and, to believe their photo album, we'd spent at least one local holiday. I was too small-minded at the time to savor any landscape that wasn't melodramatic. In fact, my single recollection has me juggling a hard-on while foraging a porn stream on my laptop and staring daggers at the ceiling, which contained or rather was a giant painting of me falling from the sky that my father, having thought my bedroom's heights an eyesore, commissioned from some trendy artist of the period.

In fact, my childhood was so cornered by the art my father bought and believed more advantageous than our furniture, it's quite likely I was brainwashed by those stationary ghouls into an artful work of human whose charms are similarly thin and geared to vex, and who, like their so-called post-conceptualist creators, thinks any matters of the heart, especially mine but anyone's will do, are too uncool to represent.

There were dirt roads everywhere we looked, but they inevitably veered not into helpful clots of trees but through endless blocks of maybe ankle-high wild grasses and the midget crops of nearby farmers.

Had it been the winter, I might have gambled, viewed the trunk as something more romantic, say the bottom of a well where Serge had fallen, and chanted, "Stay with us, buddy," or some other futile pleasantry.

If Serge had died before we reached the streets of Paris, I would have more than compensated with his slack-jawed shell. To speak somewhat frankly, every boy I've known as well as killed has struck me as his corpse's baby picture.

Still, even a mild summer day is no preservative, and dead boys aren't exactly wheels of brie, however much they might smell the same eventually.

When Serge's lonesome taps grew less important than his wheezing, I told Azmir that if he wished to fuck an ass with any sassiness at all, we should save its owner now and cross our fingers that, if anyone drove past, he would be gay enough to think someone as cute as me could do no wrong.

Azmir swerved our car onto the roadside, causing me to grasp the nearest handle and Serge to bang around and yowl inside his can.

To make the transfer look bewildering, we needed to employ a sleight of hand. While I can spin a tricky story, Serge was more than just a word on that occasion. Luckily, dust is basically a rustic fog unless you're scientific, so Azmir stomped the brakes, which blasted out a semi-decent cloud cover.

We jumped outside then coughed and blinked our way

back to the trunk, where, after leaving two or three new nasty scratches, Azmir stabbed the key into the lock. As the lid was drifting open, we grabbed two fistfuls, raised the shredding bundle, and cantered to the nearest door.

So, Serge would live to see another morning, as they say. Well, if we're to speak of what he saw in bold quotation marks, I'd guess his body might have sensed the sun, then signaled "morning" to his brain, and even that conjecture's wild since, if I'm remembering correctly, we would have needed a forensics handbook to be certain it was him.

One of Serge's eyes was getting lost in the confusion of its fattening lids. He had a boxer's coin-purse gash beneath the same eye, and his nose was blowing ruddy bubbles. One front tooth was chipped in half, and its twin, while still intact, was tumbling on his tongue until it washed up on his blobby lower lip.

He would touch the Xmas pattern on his sweater very lightly, then yelp as if the little pines were shorting outlets, so I think he had fractured ribs. Most of one black jeans leg had been torn away, baring a thigh and calf whose faded scrapes were his responsibility, and a bleeding, crooked knee that surely wasn't.

Can we agree that, had the next few hours passed routinely, I would have asked Azmir to use the Citroën's GPS and fetch the nearest doctor's office? I might have spent the hurried drive there begging Serge's pardon and surrendering, oh, money or a rain check in return for his silence on the matter.

Now, were I gay or, if you insist, entirely gay, I would have . . . well, you tell me. I'm not gay enough to know. Were I to take a guess, it would be all of the above, plus some fiery disappointment upon finding such an aftermath in such a tempting spot.

Picture a movie star who draws you to the cineplex however poor his films' reviews because you'd rather watch him change his shirt in silhouette in any context than mollify his critics. Now, recall the lavish masturbation he imposed on you, or all the time you wasted stalking him, if you went that insane.

Now, imagine it's late at night in the Marais. You're walking home from . . . what's that skeezy club . . . Le Depot, where, true to form, anyone who'd cruised you wasn't anything like him. In one last bid to meet his counterpart, you try the hotbed of Passage de Retz, and, as though its yellowed lamps were magic wands, the very actor you would die to fuck is lurking in a doorway.

He's shockingly petit, and, judging by his lumpen build, perhaps the offspring of at least one midget parent. Having arrived without an airbrush, his boney cheeks and poring eyes are geographical data in a countryside of acne, and the hand that slid thin gold bands down your imaginary finger is littered with rings and bling and scrubbing a penis you would hardly even notice otherwise.

When he spots your shadow, or rather any human shadow, he whispers, "Fuck me" or "I want to fuck you" or whatever. Once upon a time, you'd dreamt of saving him from death, but, and please be honest, now that his irksome modesty on-screen is such a head slapper, wouldn't hundreds of knife wounds serve a greater purpose, assuming the coast is clear?

Granted, that point of comparison got swept away with my effusiveness.

Point is, I'm complicated, or, rather, there's a strangely wending path between what I intend to say and what I gather I am thinking. I've always been this jumbled, even when my speech patterns employed a smaller engine and I thought about my weirdness in highly critical ways.

You'll have noticed I tell stories in a high-strung, flighty, tonally unstable rant, no sooner flashing you a secret entrance than pretending no such route exists, twittering when there's bad news, and polishing my outbursts. Flawed and mutually shortchanging as the method may be, this is the only way I know how to engage what I've done with due respect and keep you somewhat agog simultaneously.

I've gotten lost, and so have you. I'm not as witty as I wish, and you're nowhere near as patient with my heaping phrases as I evidently am.

I learned this quote-unquote exalted style of speaking from my father, who originally cooked it up after several early business trips around the Western world. He nicknamed it "the marbled swarm," which I agree is a cumbrous mouthful, and its ostensible allure received a decent portion of the credit for accruing his, now my, billions.

One night when I was thirteen years old, he passed along the recipe, which I should have written down, but I'd just come home zonked on one too many hits of Ecstacy, and he was tipsy from a course of Chardonnays, so he could barely have enunciated the instructions in any case.

If you're curious, memory tells me that this voice was generated from a dollop of the haughty triple-speak British royals employ to keep their hearts reclusive, some of the tricked, incautious slang that dumbs down young Americans, a dollop of the stiff, tongue-twisting, jammed-up sentence structure and related terseness that comes with being German, some quisling, dogmatic Dutch retorts, and a few other international ingredients I didn't catch, which is the central problem with my scrappier version, all of which my father blended smoothly into his mellifluous French.

The marbled swarm is spoken at a taxing pace in trains

of sticky sentences that round up thoughts as broadly as a vacuum. Ideally, its tedium is counteracted by linguistic decorations, with which the speaker can design the spiel to his requirements. The result, according to this mode's inventor, is that one's speech becomes an entity as open-ended as the air it fills and yet as dangerous to travel as a cluttered, unlit room in which someone has hidden, say, a billion euros.

My father used the marbled swarm to . . . well, I was going to say become a wealthy man, and that is true, but to say he ruined my life would be as accurate.

My marbled swarm is more of an atonal, fussy bleat—somewhat marbled yet far too frozen tight and thinned by my loquaciousness to do the swarming it implies. Still, it seems to be a sleeper hit with guys my age and younger, or at least with the majority who tune in once they're weakened by my stunning looks.

For this fan base, my dry, chiseled meanderings seem to add a fleeting touch of magic to a face whose knee-jerk beauty might be too digestible. Long story short, had my father not half taught me to talk like this, I might instead be leering up at you from the cover of *Vogue* or, ugh, *Tétu*.

To people who knew my father well, say Azmir and several others you'll be meeting, I am little more than his subpar impressionist—a miscast, bargain-basement chip off the veritable old block, à la, say, Hayden Christensen's wooden rendition of Anakin Skywalker.

I won't refute that I'm a busker of my father's genius. Still, to give myself some credit, his wizardry was called for by his dull, unhelpful visage, which was frequently compared to Gérard Jugnot's, if you know him, whereas it could be argued I need a far less charismatic soundtrack.

As for how my cover version sits with you who lack that crucial additive, I really couldn't guess and ultimately fear the worst, but . . . fine, I'll go as blunt as the sound bite to which my life will be reduced by the same journalists who fashion headlines from its trail of circumstantial evidence.

I'm what you'd call a cannibal, or, rather, I'm the fig-urehead, curator, human bankroll, and most willing if not wanton of a clique of cannibals, our exact number depending on who happens to be horny and/or hungry and/or situated in Paris or still alive at any given moment.

Christophe, mid-forties, is primarily a sadist, and were embroidering the lexicon of human screams a sport, he'd be a gladiator, but, at least until we're jailed, he's best known to those who've never met him as the cosmetic surgeon of choice for French celebrities and government officials.

His son Claude—and that doubled name is problematic, I agree—was a nineteen-year-old ballet dancer who became a member of our team for several hours, but since sixty of his

kilos were on the menu at the time, his designation as a chum
is strictly for sticklers.

François, fifty-something, is a noted chef whose "bitter"
cooking packs the four-star restaurant L'Astrance. At first, he
saw mankind as a bonanza, as ground too hallowed not to
break, and he used our dinner prattle as a critique, but, after
mastering his spin on what he calls this "cult" cuisine, he's
much more tolerable personally.

His sons Olivier and Didier round—or, in Didier's case,
and, come to think of it, Olivier's as well, rounded—out our
inner circle.

Olivier, my age but Japanese, was hungrier for gory films
than body parts. He would watch them so incessantly without
uncalled-for blinks or bathroom breaks that, although I never
asked, I assume he saw the tactile aspect of our cookouts as a
further step in entertainment history akin to IMAX 3D.

Didier struck inattentive strangers as a kind of Pugsly
trapped within some all-male Addams Family, but, since he
lived for everyone's protection in a cage, he was really more
our mascot. By this moment in my story, both Olivier and he
have been digested, unless, that is, you ever stumble on my
chateau and note two quadrants of the yard that seem peculiarly indented, in which case bingo.

Barring François, the others stay around for dinner to be
social more than anything else.

I won't claim I don't enjoy our aperitif-like orgies, and, if you could view the CDRs, you might quibble with my need to watch the rapes with folded arms, but I would defy you to call me a dispassionate wallflower.

Everyone knows Shakespeare's bon mot wherein a loved one is colluded with a summer's day. Well, I will hazard an off-shoot whereby the so-called loved one is a kid like Serge who isn't lovable at all, and the summer's day is instead a flower, say a rose too odorous to leave unsniffed in, oh, the Luxembourg Gardens.

For some, the drives to dock one's face in boys or plants are interchangeable. My urge, you see, is not to flavor my receptors with some pretty thing's most scented chasm. Rather, my nosedives bind a bee's gluttonous raiding with the scrutinizing glances of a scissors-laden florist.

So, as I handed Serge some tissues, ice, an Evian, and one more painkiller than was provident to swallow, and even as I feared my colleagues' whining when I brought this mess into my loft, I personally found him far more pornographic, if such a scoured term can handle that.

He'd downed the pain pills, wrapped two ice cubes in a tissue and clamped the bundle to his eye, but reaching for his knee transformed his ribs into tormentors, so I was icing that injury while steadying the leg for all intents and purposes.

Serge had the wishy-washy leg of someone fractionally his

age, with skin as giving as a sandy beach and so puddled on the bone, a slap might well have splashed white glops all over everything, which I would guess sounds nauseating if you think of legs as more than entrées in the making.

Serge might have thought I was caressing him were I not just thrilled enough to have deliberately massaged that leg, at least unconsciously.

"When I'm depressed, everything's a joke to me, and no one thinks my jokes are funny, and I'm depressed right now, just to warn you," he said.

Back when Serge was a more kempt, undamaged fashion plate, the gloomy tenor of his voice had raised my eyebrow in suspicion. It felt accessorized, as fake as the elation in a clown's honking falsetto, but whether Serge was still a broadcast or was digging deep seemed immaterial.

"It will no doubt please you that these pills appear to be working," he said.

When I'm turned on, as you'd put it, and I was—even if my mind feels like a boulder resting on your shoulders, you'd love what I was feeling—I can sound unusually off the cuff, even kiss-ass. Still, keep in mind my praise is never kinder to its wellspring than a classic film's ten thousandth rave review.

Anyway, I lavished many adjectives on Serge's leg, albeit terms more suited to a golden-throated butcher than his sweetheart.

Mostly for effect, I gripped the tattered jeans and ripped them open to his belt—and it's fortunate that when one's strength is taxed, a strained expression can look horny if one adds at least a crooked smile—then snuck one hand inside his underwear, which were black and flecked with tiny skulls if that seems relevant.

I told Serge if he were worried that his negligible penis would undercut him, he absolutely shouldn't, and that I was lingering and fingering because its toastiness encouraged me.

"Thanks, I guess," he whispered, then, perhaps undone by that reminder of his childishness, he started crying. Technically, I think you would have called it a wail or even bray.

Azmir, who had been studying the road inside a bobbing, skull-shaped discotheque juiced by some kerplunking playlist on his iPod, heard a trace of Serge's bawling, fished out an earphone, and yelled at me to turn him down.

"I just wanted you to rape me," Serge squawked. "Not once but even endlessly. I don't mean 'endlessly' because I think I'm worth the work involved. I just thought or dreamt or what the fuck that when you said 'Not yet,' you meant a month or even years from now."

I told him "yet" had meant tomorrow, but, were he to count it down in screams instead of days, it would feel more like a year.

"It's not that I'm some giant fan of sex," Serge continued.

"Its blaze of glory status is the world's most bullshit lie, if you ask me, even bigger than the hoax involving Santa Claus, but rape has . . . I don't know, a kind of . . . something else, at least when you imagine it."

I asked if, to his mind, being raped so frequently had coined this favoritism.

"Well, there are these seven . . . wait, nine guys I used to chat with who, if I know them, and I don't, probably tell their friends they raped some Emo loser," he said.

"It's true when we were instant messaging, they were all, like, 'Rape, rape, pound your ass, and blah blah blah, you little whore.' But when they saw . . . that I was serious, it was all, like, 'You shouldn't cut yourself, you're really nice,' and then they'd get my face alone and maybe jack off in my mouth, if I was lucky.

"I just . . . was happy that you didn't act all psychiatric, and . . . you remind me of my brother, which I know is sick, but . . . God, I sound like the Elephant Man."

At that, the car swerved sideways, rocking and skidding down the roadside. Azmir, who'd started yelling in some language that sounds scarier than French, held the steering wheel with one hand, turned around, and threw a punch that squashed the racket out of Serge's face, then followed it with three or four more blows that left the boy's head lolling on the car's rear deck and splashed a bloody image of his face over the tinted glass above.

There are experts in the field of art who claim a child or alien from outer space would know van Gogh is greater than realistic painters without knowing he was a suffering lunatic. Not that growing up in a museum gave me expertise, but Serge's swelling, slushy face made his cuter one seem too conformist, and I swear his pain and trouble breathing weren't the differentials.

I tugged out several tissues, grabbed some ice cubes, and made two chilly wads, then dug them into his palms, leaned those hands against his lips and nostrils, and asked the gory mess if Serge could speak.

"I think . . . with a lot of effort . . . yes," replied a soggy whisper.

I suggested that, if he had questions, he should pose them now rather than later for reasons I would spare him.

"Where am I going?" he asked.

I explained that he would shortly meet some friends of mine, and, were past events with like beginnings symptomatic, there would follow an impromptu show spotlighting him.

He might be nude or over-dressed in one of several dozen costumes that are saved for such occasions and whose simulacrums range from a convincing grizzly bear to vintage military garb to all variety of slutty drag. Thus ritzed up, he might dance and sing and tell some jokes and read poetry aloud and give each of us a lap dance.

Ideally, my friends would then be starry-eyed enough to rape him as an encore, which, according to the definition of "rape" I was employing, included both the violent penetration he would expect as well as creepier acts that he would dislike tremendously and barely live through.

We would pause to get some air, then reconvene at his chateau, where the raping would continue and, given how much less we'd have to work with, escalate and run its course, growing murderous so casually that he would likely find the two brands of close attention indistinguishable.

After he'd died, or, rather, once we tired of torturing his likeness, he would find his way onto a kitchen counter. There, the most perverted of my friends would rape his stiffening cadaver while the rest of us dismembered it beneath him like lumberjacks who won't abide some tree hugger.

We might take a little field trip to his bedroom, explore his ex-belongings for a while, and debate what they revealed about him. No doubt a shower would be warranted, after which, refreshed, we would drift back into the kitchen.

One friend would butcher, hew, and snip his body parts into a selective dozen at the most and then prepare a meal featuring his high points as the aperitif, main course, and possibly dessert.

I might raid the gallery of family photographs along the chateau's staircase and create a table setting, or we might screen a video of him in costume from the night before. We'd marvel, gossip, and trade anecdotes about him, clean our plates, wash them, and then never think of him again for as long as we lived.

"Being excessively earnest, or so I'm always told, I wouldn't know if you were kidding if I cared," Serge said.

Given how fiercely Azmir had punched him, I said I wasn't shocked, and if his brain was hemorrhaging—and his ennui at my story was suspicious—what lay ahead for him was subject to truncation.

"I was joking," Serge said. "I told you no one ever gets it."

I said if he were queried out, I hoped to make short use of his dwindling capacities. Then I withdrew the group of envelopes I'd stolen from Claude's bedroom, extracted the letter I'd previously read, and held it a reasonable distance from his face.

I asked if what was written there were true.

His good eye read the paper haltingly then stalled around the midway point, branching off the page and stilling in his lap, whether from retinal inertia or small penis worries or the upshot of brain damage, I'll never really know.

"Ask Claude," he said nebulously.

I asked him to confirm that he had written it.

"Write it," he said. "You think . . . I wrote myself a letter about . . . me?"

I told him I was confused.

"My face hurts," he said, and, glancing worriedly at the back of Azmir's head, he bit his lower lip extremely gently then attempted, I believe, not to move enough to harm himself sufficiently to cry enough to bring more pain upon him.

I'm sparing you the convoluted turns of phrase my voice accumulates whenever I feel pressured to create a sympathetic portrait of . . . well, anyone, and that includes myself.

Still, I know a dry approach will leave Serge unrealistic, so I'll avoid this scene and simply say we had a brief, heart-tugging, if you wish, disintegrated, shedding conversation until his chin fell on his chest in what could charitably be called sleep.

I tend to think dying people tell the truth, although I don't know why truth would magically become their native language, and one should never underestimate sappy, brain-washing movies.

I'll consolidate the things I learned from Serge into a tentative report that virtually every word from his and Jean-Paul's lips before I'd cleaned his out had been a lie.

To feel the impact of this mindfuck, try imagining my voice is something more concrete and physically imposing than the book I hope it will inject then spend eternity in print. Let's say . . . it's a chateau, since that setting is still fresh.

Let's say while you've been reading or, as it turns out, believing you were reading, you've been hanging out in my chateau attentively enough to have found your way into that hidden thoroughfare I outlined, or, in this case, a confidential, wandering sentence.

If you're with me, my words and what they've detailed to this point would constitute the chateau's furniture and so forth. I would be the building's architect, and my story, such as it is, would form the floor plan. Serge would be the guest of honor who has suddenly gone missing or, more fruitfully, has been replaced when none of you were looking with a mannequin that duplicates his physical appearance.

In other words, everything you've read thus far was more mischievous than you imagined. Since the writing hasn't altered, and a quick recheck would find it just as stiff and slightly out of touch as ever, there's no reason to stop reading, or, returning to the chateau allegory, to cease hanging out like you've been doing all along.

Still, you're advised that what you see around you—walls, if you're hallucinating, or certain facts, if you're my readers—are potentially encrypted—with passageways if you're "chateau" guests, or subtexts if you're with me—and certain givens such as who scarred Serge's body, how Claude died if he's deceased, who was with me in the hidden tunnels, Claire's existence, who gave Serge a sex life if he had one, and so forth, are now analogies at best.

I'll debug those lingering confusions when or if the time is right, and, for now, you need only tag along behind me with a smidgen more intimacy than ever.

I've never read a decent novel in my life unless skimming fifteen pages of Houellbecq's *Platform* to make conversation counts, but, as I understand it, when one reads novels, it's the realness of the characters that seals your eyes between the covers, whereas the world they supposedly inhabit is closer to a compass, built just carefully enough to help you keep your bearings.

If I'm right, then I'll suggest you try to get things backward. The Serge you think you know to some degree was just his body's force of habit, and that custom has been broken.

Serge was like those tombs they keep discovering in Egypt where every bit of gold was sacked and cleared out centuries ago by robbers, and what the robbers left behind is on its way to some museum. The tombs' cave-ins are braced with timbers, and their filthy tunnels have been vacuumed into hallways, and now there's nothing left to do but charge tourists an arm and a leg to file through empty basements.

Serge was just a given name. In fact, I'll strip his body of that moniker and call him # 7, if that helps, which is to say whoever used his Emo premise or how he might have wrinkled up and sagged however many years from now is as inconsequential as the light source coursing through some chandelier.

7 was meat, a veritable cow cursed to live complexly like a boy, as in the children's stories, his clothes as tacked on as a circus dog's tuxedo, and, whether you can see him through my specializing eyes or not, they're the only contact lens that can get you safely through the rest of this.

Before the ordinary building at 118 rue de Turenne was remodeled by my father, it housed the oldest shoe factory in Paris. The amplifying taste for footwear rubber-stamped by the likes of Vans and Nike had long since dashed its workforce into a skeleton crew, but before the geriatric owner swiped my father's credit card, it was still rattling along.

Our home had previously and always been a mansion several stuffy blocks from the Eiffel Tower, until, that is, my mother was discovered on the kitchen floor, zapped off her feet by an alleged brain tumor that had gone suspiciously undetected by her doctors, or so my father said.

As time crawls, I've come to realize the subtitling my father gave our lives was a ruse no less designed to keep our views in check than the security guard–like monsters that evil stepmothers litter in their bedtime stories.

Nonetheless, my mother's death left him disconsolate, or, rather, inspired the diagnosis he gave to his performance—which, to be frank, seems increasingly bloodless in retrospect.

Our mansion, which he'd pooh-poohed as too parochial in girth and stature to foreground his giant art collection, or, rather, the bulky two or three dozen giant artworks he deemed investments, was now additionally denounced as an engine of unbearable memories.

After several months, the shoe factory was dialed back into a stack of spacious lofts, and my father rearranged our new, chopped-up family in its layers.

My father commandeered the top-floor-cum-penthouse. My younger brother, Alfonse, was installed just below him on the third floor, and my loft sat just below his on the building's second level.

Alfonse will be puzzling to epitomize, not because anything about him would turn descriptive prose into a vampire's mirror, but difficult like reassembling a plane crash. Perhaps I'll dash him off for now as a dedicated fan of manga since he read Japanese comix so incessantly the volumes might as well have been his shirt collars, although "fan" sounds far too freelance.

He was more a kind of mermaid stalled between his illustrated heroes' printed pages, where he longed to fly around on jetpack shoes and switch genders with a button push, and our heftier dimension, where he survived but thought himself fatally ill suited.

Hundreds of utopian self-portraits were crammed into his hard drive, where, using Paint or Adobe Photoshop, he'd pried frames from the fatal scenes in some cartoon or childish film, then spent hours replacing the Road Runner's Wolf or the freeze-dried Hans Solo with a pancake of himself.

Once while we were playing Truth or Dare, he chose truth and, when asked to be his death's designer, picked a hit-and-run accident by steamroller. Most effectively for your reading purposes, he haunted several online chat rooms full of equally withdrawn kids and lying predators who lionized paper thinness and called themselves squish junkies.

In the real world of school desks and sidewalks, Alfonse had his distant admirers, most of them too old to qualify comfortably as friends. It would be safe to say I was his only friend, had our behavior when together not misused the classic meaning of that term.

Better to say were I the movie star my telegenic looks and presumptive manner warranted, he might have been some actor hired to portray me in my flashbacks. He treated every brush with me as though it was a precious opportunity to learn my latest tics and traits, then play them back like I were his aerobics instructor.

Consequently, I saw Alfonse as my imprecise reflection, and the portrait of him that would occasionally materialize within the wash of my devoted likeness took the form of physical discrepancies or misinterpretations that were too piecemeal to appraise.

Alfonse's only quote-unquote friends lived in the violent bric-a-brac universe of websites and chat rooms traveled by the squish junkies, the majority of whom preferred to smash cute things than be trampled, so whether they were friends or mutual conveniences is certainly debatable.

My father stuck Alfonse with a nanny, who, at the age of twenty-four, still had the bowl haircut, jejune school clothes, and puerile interests of someone newly postpubescent. Within days of being hired, Mon Petit Bichette, as he called himself, quit dressing and deporting like his prior ward-cum-molestee and colonized my brother's superhero look, Japanomania, and the general behavior Alfonse had watered down from mine.

When Mon Petit Bichette wasn't sexting Alfonse, tailoring his pants into a second skin, or recycling his dirty socks as tea cozies—and that is not a case of me exaggerating— he occupied the loft below mine on the first floor, where his nightly blasts of disco-era Claude François and hooting recitations of the songs' feebleminded lyrics would cause my furniture to move around my loft very slightly, like grazing cows.

As for the building's ground floor, I've never picked its rusty lock, if you believe that, but then again I've never stuck my head in Sacre Coeur for much the same reason. Just as I needn't see a bunch of gilded Jesus statues to visualize an extra-special church, whatever's buried in the dust down there undoubtedly deserves it.

Each loft was designed, if one can call a sterile, subdivided stretch of low-lit rectangular nothingness a design, by the architect Philippe Starck and featured a scatter of his artsy, uncomfortable furniture.

In the huge swaths of wall and floor space left unchecked by Starck's concept, my father laid out obstacle courses of his art holdings—exhibitions he claimed to have curated with such precision that the theme of each mini-collection would have caused it to be titled with our respective first names had the building been open to the public.

For a time, I was certain the lofts additionally disguised some creepy underpinnings—evil eye–like nitty-gritty, if you will—diabolic minutia that my nervous system sensed even as its symptoms proved impalpable—and whose existence I was to neither establish nor disprove until my father's sudden, pell-mell death.

An elevator, or, rather, a trendy sculptor's perfect replication of *The Shining*'s lift, but painted red inside instead of filled with blood, would drop Alfonse and me to street level or lift us to my father's digs for rare communal meals whenever he decided to admit he was in town.

Bizarrely, my father's floor had been abridged into a small and strangely shaped apartment that hardly gouged the yawning volume at its disposal, an anomaly he claimed was neither fanciful nor frugal, but rather fallout from having to share his level with the gargantuan equipment that warmed and cooled the building.

Like Alfonse in one regard, I've never had friends, not in the "give a shit" sense, not even when I was too young to have selected them myself. Thus, having tons of downtime wherein to stage my wildest daydreams likely fast-tracked the internal monologuist you've begun to get to know.

I had liked Alfonse with a perfect lack of passion until he colluded with his nanny. Well, "like" might be too strong a word. Admired objectively, let's say. Let's say his beauty might have garnered him a fan base cruisier than mine, were he not more garbled by stylistics and forged from less epicurean materials.

Due to my father's wealth, ego, philanthropy, and conniving grip on words, he moved in starry social circles. There were rumors at one time that he'd fucked Isabelle Adjani, the once ethereal actress turned plastic surgeon's monster. Although my father seemed insulted by this premise—even then, Adjani's buckling, placated face required a fog machine to be puffing in her photo sessions—it seemed quite a coincidence that she had famously retired for nine months just before Alfonse debuted in the arms of my thin, grimacing mother.

Alfonse's outermost layer preserved the young Adjani's vaunted snowy skin, starless black hair, the same startled, chocolate eyes that infatuated costars or stared convincingly through windows of insane asylums, the congested lips, and, like the actress in her least successful films and unlike me, he struck everyone who cared to give our family feedback as looking slightly too refrigerated.

Had Alfonse not channeled his neurosis into a frenetic self-escape plan wherein my affectations formed the hatch, he might have grown depressed enough to find the little something extra to defrost his stiltedness in Emo's throttling wardrobe. Without a stylish herd in which to camouflage his weak links, he dressed like his manga heroes might have dressed were they inflated like balloons, which is to say dorkily.

Alfonse might even be alive, sitting in a pose almost identical to mine, pretending to write his own memoir, his hand and pen jiggling one hair's breadth above an untouched page, but then I might still be a suffocated nympho, so, ultimately, I have to say it's more productive that he's dead.

Point is, until a series of events I'm preparing to address, he'd always bugged me with the feckless dedication of a housefly. But, on what seemed an average afternoon as I half observed my brother's stagey reenactment of who I'd been moments before, it occurred to me that his playback was somehow . . . clingier.

It seemed not the royal performance to which I'd grown lackadaisically accustomed, but something more daring, an act less bent on piecing me together through pinpoint accuracy or plagiarizing my reserve than geared to undermine the very fuss that caused my personality to barely surface in the first place.

Previously, rare nods or smiles would be enough to keep my mirror image ambient. Now, any sign of my approval caused Alfonse to mutiny, diversify, and grow ever more technically inaccurate. I felt less flattered by and independent of his sequel than challenged to keep up with its liberties.

I began to see him as a stripper haggling with my equivalents. Were he not spoiled rotten like myself, I might have stuffed a wad of euros in his belt, then . . . well, do what exactly was the problem.

The weakest part of his impression had always been its hollowness, although I'll grant that void was not particularly his fault. I'm no extrovert, even when I'm yelling, "Die, you piece of shit," and every precocious, news-making ten-year-old "new Mozart" in the world is eventually discovered to be a piano-playing parrot.

Alfonse modeled the mechanics of my presence, but while his forgery was dutiful, it lacked the telltale oomph that came with my perverseness.

This lost ingredient, while piddling in the grander scheme of me—think of the line between the "car" an actor "drives" into a "wall" and the car-like prop in which his lifelike dummy burns alive—and which had never seemed a flaw in his depiction when my viewing was more casual, now outstripped my loneliness as the major reason I was not unhappy to bump into him.

In order to one-up my brother's mating dance, I undertook a bit of research into the sex practices of odd couples going back for centuries. Strangely at the time, if quite predictably to you, I seemed to feel the coziest and greatest kinship with a thread of history's most heinous boy-killers, in particular the doings of one obscure but fascinating German individual.

Klaus Freeh was a particle scientist who thought if he could humanize his grasp of nanoparticulates, he might become the world's first genius cannibal. Fatally stabbed by the very first boy-slash-future-slab-of-meat he abducted, he left behind a notebook in which he'd repeatedly sketched and expounded upon "the perfect human storm," as he described it—a body type that, according to his findings, would both render art superfluous and, were Germany a jungle, send rivulets of spit down its population's teeth.

I should add out of fairness that his theories have been razored into kookyville by every learned historian for whom the cannibal is second nature, their opinion being that Freeh was just a sick fuck, and no evidence suggests that human taste buds are as picky as he posited.

Need I even say that, at least in his scanned drawings I found online, had some fashion designer thought to translate them into couture, Alfonse's body could have smoothed them into leotards.

In the weeks since Alfonse muscled through the sheen of my resemblance, he'd been cast as the romantic lead in every reverie I concocted. There wasn't a harmful prank or convoluted fuckfest that his imaginary figment hadn't rehearsed to a Kubrickian finish, but it wasn't until Freeh's ill-starred masterstroke hit home that I'd made my final cut.

I hadn't chewed and swallowed anyone as of the period in question, but I'd felt and thought everything violent and ruinous of my clothing this side of actually combusting into a pack of hungry tigers every time I got a hard-on.

I'd never even cooked myself an omelet. The illusory skin wedged between my fairyland of teeth would puncture like a bubble, tear from each anatomy with a pleasant-sounding rip, and be transformed by my obedient taste buds from knotty, sopping flesh and muscle into a favorite food, which at that time was spaghetti bolognaise.

Having preemptively tagged myself as gay, I was still too in thrall to the same-sex party line that an acrobatic fuck was the mom and pop of making out, and any partnership more offbeat, much less one that challenged laws both French and biblical, constituted one's self-hatred.

By the way, I just had an awful thought—one you've no doubt been musing on for pages. Christ, I do go on, is what I thought, and my fingers literally tensed above the keyboard.

Rather than offer you some insincere apology, I'll make a slightly premature admission that, if you think I've dragged my story from its bearings—namely, the serpentine chateau, its secretive owner, his doomed son Serge—and that I've lost my proper place within it as your talky host—you're . . . half wrong.

Yes, this recent blather is a strike against my toned-down marbled swarm, but it's also an assurance of my honesty, even when, as I've come to know and you will understand eventually, I was less finding my true self back then or living day to day in the democratic sense than enacting a "life" no more incipient than a toy's.

If I'd taken I don't know how many words of caution in my life and spun my insights thusly but within earshot of a reputable psychologist . . . well, I have no idea.

For his twelfth birthday, Alfonse asked me on what amounted to a date. His chosen getaway was Die!!Die!!Color!!!, an annual convention wherein the newest manga, anime, candy-colored gadgets, and other Japanese playthings with internal hard drives were unveiled to thousands of Asiatic Parisians and freeloaders like my brother in the Parc des Expositions.

Billed and barely marketed for years as your basic Japan Expo, the rechristened Die!!Die!!Color!!! had a screaming, jam-packed advertising scheme to match its switched-out title, and one could not have traveled via metro to or from Bastille, Belleville, or other hipster centrals in many months without trying to decode its vast, headache-inducing posters.

Thus, I pictured an event traipsed by coolness-seeking fashionistas, its aisles as wan and hushed by pretense as the runways of Chanel or Gareth Pugh, and I gambled that Alfonse would rein his usual Narcissus at the pond routine into, at best, a pitiable nerdiness that might, at worst, cause me to blush occasionally.

The only catch involved keeping my newly motivated hands off Alfonse's freshly gripping figure and folded in my lap throughout the car trip to and fro, during which we'd be dangerously soundproofed in the rear compartment of the limousine my father had unhelpfully rented for the occasion.

Luckily, the route took us through Paris and not a Saudi Arabian desert-scape at night.

Vacations aside, I've been a hard-core Parisian since I was born the way dinosaurs stuck in tar pits might as well be fossils. So, once Azmir had eased our road hog through the cunning intersection where rue de Turenne crosses, kills, and swipes the cars from rue de Bretagne, then somehow squeezed onto the tiny rue Vieille du Temple, its close-knit, historically important views enlivened my Olympian detachment, and I fended off the hanky-panky building up on our respective tongues and fingers with the almost unbroken gushing of a tour guide.

You witnessed my skills in this regard when I bent poor Serge's ear vis-à-vis the trove of his backyard, and my methodology was near identical in this case, but with baroque and art nouveau façades, and the wordier superlatives they portended, in place of samey trees.

By the time Azmir off-loaded us at Parc des Expositions, I had waxed, emblazoned, and spit-polished a fairly average set of boulevards into a virtual Champs-Élysées at Christmas, and Alfonse, who found any city without flying cabs and giant, evil robots severely lacking, was my numbed, sensibly tight-lipped hostage.

I'd accompanied my father to the very same convention hall years before for a like-minded fair at which the tourism bureaus from hundreds of unpopular countries hoped to sell French travel agents on the blueness of their lakes and the alluringly slight differences in the layouts of their golf courses.

I believe he had a cockamamie scheme to turn the art he'd bought into the centerpiece of a museum in some country so bereft of wonders that it would be a major tourist attraction by default. As was usually the case when he hoped to close a deal, I'd been drafted in as his accoutrement in hopes of dazzling sentimentalists or pedophiles with his prestigious genes, which, of course, weren't his to begin with.

All I can remember is my hair was patted to an oily clump and that my ass was groped surreptitiously so often and invasively by prospective clients that I suffered muscle cramps in my posterior for days, requiring the aid of an osteopath, who also took my disadvantage as an opportunity to help himself.

Perhaps were I a physicist, I could explain why Die!! Die!!Color!!!, although no more towering or spread out than the dolled-up shantytown that formed the so-called International Salon du Monde, made the same convention hall that could have covered several Notre Dames with room to spare feel as claustrophobic as a crawl space.

I've never been the kind of person who gyrates into toy stores, not even when my love of things was new and sloppy. After years of hobbling stiffly through Nuit Blanches and theme parks, I began to answer invitations to hit the town with, No, thank you. I have an allergy to stimulus.

François, the most piquant of my cannibal associates, once remarked upon the irony of my apeirophobia, as one specialist has diagnosed the problem, given my insistence on talking as though I represented the EU in some unofficial capacity.

While my fear of excess stimulus predates my . . . let's say "punk" adaptation of the marbled swarm, it's quite possible the swarm's repellant quality appealed to me unconsciously.

Fortunately, just as Alfonse began to tow me by one sweating hand into the fair's storm front of clogged and supersaturated shopping aisles, the word "plank" was shrieked by someone or other in the thick crowd tussling around us.

After some jostling in our vicinity, Alfonse was mob-hugged by two . . . Asian, perhaps . . . things . . . female, I guessed at first . . . or maybe young drag queens, I wasn't sure . . . who had apparently recognized him from the avatar he used when chatting in the "squish junkie" enclaves I mentioned earlier.

Plank was Alfonse's 2-D alter ego, and, if the glittering block letters on their badges were any indication, the intruders' "names" were Slat and Log.

These "Flatsos"—the term that I would later learn was proper for their artificial species—seemed less to have been born and raised than magically peeled from the cover of an especially creative manga, then resized to teenage height by some miraculous process that left their torsos no thicker than guitar cases.

In place of heads of hair, they wore cardboard coiffures shaped like Napoleon's sideways helmet and painted the red of roosters' mohawks. The curving tops were scissored into uneven saw teeth or maybe sun rays that were symbolic of the Flatsos' unkempt hair.

The duo's outfits appeared to be ankle-length pinafores ironed as flat as paper fans then starched, dipped in vats of liquid lollipop, then somehow crammed over two real bodies without collapsing their rib cages.

The truly disconcerting aspect, even to a skeptic like myself, were the optical illusions that some makeup artist had fashioned from their faces.

I have yet to grow a wrinkle, so my bathroom cabinet remains as spotless as a prisoner's, and I don't know about cosmetics or how it is that seventy-something Catherine Deneuve still looks fifty-something. Thus, I can't tell you why Slat and Log's faces appeared from certain angles to have no more terrain or substance than a presidential portrait on a commemorative plate.

Of course, Alfonse, to whom the first dimension promised, well, virtually everything, was beyond enamored of these handmade slips of human and overeager to resemble them. So, before I knew it, the pair had hustled him away toward some Flatso recruitment booth, and I was inching far behind them on my skidding shoes.

Once when I was still an only child and my father was quote-unquote friendly with Isabelle Adjani, I was forced to accompany them down the red carpet at the Festival de Cannes while two firing squads of paparazzi used the flash attachments on their cameras as automatic weapons, knocking down their roped enclosure to surround us, all the while yelling, "Little boy, is your father fucking her?" over and over in hundreds of foreign accents at once. In that case, I literally fainted and was carried into the theater like a dead infant prop by Isabelle.

If you're a certain kind of person, you might have seen the very shots of my humiliating moment on her official website, which I will mention she has conveniently mislabeled as among her greatest roles.

Does that convey my trauma? Shall I boringly compare myself to the biblical Egyptian spearmen tripping over themselves in the gushy mud and piles of flopping fish between the Red Sea's reconvening halves? I don't believe I can do this.

If vampire movies hadn't been the franchise of that year, and were wastrel fashion models and feeble-looking bands not so incredibly in vogue, and if a wary-eyed pallor were not, as a consequence, the diamond in the rough of facial options, my sad state might have turned the single-minded nerds and fops moseying around me into Good Samaritans.

My brother and his Flatsos had collaged themselves into the crowd. My agonizing progress was more an aftermath of others' clumsy shoulders than any effort from my fishtailing feet, when my eyes spotted a snatch of white, which I managed to squint into a handwritten sign. It was Scotch-taped to a metal folding chair that had been plunked down in the middle of the aisle, and my name was scrawled across the sheet and underlined with a wobbly arrow pointing to the left.

Given that my name is an invention, or, to paraphrase my mother at her most stoned, a magic group of letters whose implications are the key to everything on earth when one is tripping balls, and, thus, a term that, until I inspire something, refers to me and me only, and seeing that the sign, as unimpressive as it was, sought to edge me off the horrifying thoroughfare, I took its unknown scribbler at his word more than I would have otherwise.

After squeezing through a gap of space between two booths, I found myself inside a kind of gulley, created by the boulder-like rear portions of the booths that formed the aisle I'd just escaped and its immediate neighbor.

Sitting cross-legged with its back against a booth that dwarfed the others in its soaring height and flabby build and gulping down a Kronenbourg was one of Alfonse's Flatso comrades, or, rather, its recovering human.

If not for the "Log" badge now pinned to an old Nirvana T-shirt, its heavy, oblate makeup and outlandish hat of toothy hair might have pegged it as, oh, one of those die-hard soccer fans who paint their favorite team's logo on their faces to . . . well, I have no idea.

"Want one," it asked, extracting a bottle from the frayed six-pack at his side.

By the way, I won't transcribe this creature's voice into mine then throw the poor results into its mouth, except to note its voice was lower than the squeaks it used to court my brother. My one concession is to make its mind sound very simple, which it was.

I rarely drink alcohol, apart from the odd toast from which it would be rude to abstain or when dining with cannibal associates, for the simple reason that, in layman's terms, it makes me horny, or what I define as famished, which is not to say I didn't grab then finish off the beer in one humongous swallow.

"If you want to fuck your brother, he's in there," Log said, patting the monumental booth behind it, "or you could fuck me and get around a lot of bullshit."

I'm far too stiff when drunk to cause a messy scene, but my limited ability to self-edit is laid to even greater ruin. For instance, were you not filtered from this moment by its status as a recollection, and were a single bout of horniness not enough to burn me out for days, I might have slurred something to the effect of all of the above.

Having seen my share of junk that artists claimed as their hard and brilliant work, I thought the booth, or what

I'd thought a booth, might be a sculpture, arte povera most likely, or perhaps a tower crane that, having done its part to build and fluff the booths around it, was hastily wrapped in a blanket of black plastic in hopes of looking less unsightly.

By then, Log had dipped its fingers in the mushy tower's sheath and withdrawn a flap, creating an impromptu doorway in which I cautiously docked my face.

Inside, there was a gloomy shapeless room with crinkled, slightly caved-in walls. A single track light glared up from the floor, and the only furniture were two chairs of the metal folding type that had braced the aisle's handwritten sign.

In one of the chairs sat a man I recognized both as a friend of my father's and, from flipping through magazines and TV channels, as François Tirel, a famous chef at the restaurant L'Astrance, although I couldn't recall having spoken more than a thoughtless word of greeting or farewell to him.

I'd only noted him at all because each time we'd coincided, his eyes would fasten onto mine then dig around vehemently, as though his eyesight was a power drill and I their padlock.

"Were you to squeeze yourself through there," he said, pointing at a second gap or lapse in the room's most puckered wall, "but you shouldn't just yet, you would shortly find your delicious brother, but why not sit and get to know yourself first."

It can't remotely surprise you that the word "delicious," and the mystery of what made it seem appropriate, is what

inspired me to maneuver inside, trailed by Log, who continued past and through the gap François had asked me to regard
with patience.

"My younger son, Didier, for the record," François said.
"No doubt he's thrown himself at you. Were I not here to
cull our better interests, I might shock you by redoubling his
offer. Still, I fear that were his face not divined into a Flatso's, your next few words would not be 'What an awesome
dad' but 'Why is it I feel a new nostalgia for the era of the
guillotine?'

"In the opinion of five—count them, five—pediatricians,
and not just do-gooder French clinic workers, but two American specialists and a Russian Nobel Prize recipient, there is a
curlicue among my son's synapses, a genetic mishap I attribute
to my ex-wife, the insane bitch, that routes the over-energy
that grips all boys his age into some organ in the body that
feeds his efflorescing genitalia.

"Thus, the impulse to, say, gather action figures or skateboard everywhere is instead a warped addiction wherein his
ass is a collection plate and every penis on earth no matter
how minuscule is a valuable collector's item.

"Have I, in dire circumstances, blotted out his features
with a pillow then screwed the liberated body senseless, yes,
and were I the type of S and M practitioner who hands his
prostitutes a leather hood the same way you or I might offer

ours a cocktail, Alfonse and you might be at home right now instead of . . .

"Still, rather than complete that thought and stretch this conversation, I'll leave the thinness of your smile untouched for now and reaffirm my offer should you ever find his ugliness subversive by some miracle.

"More important, I have unpleasant news. It seems your life of recent months has been a fairy tale, and you one of its two unwitting characters, and I happen to be privy to the thinking that inspired it. While in most cases, say, when a child grows old enough to know J.R.R. Tolkien was just staring at a typewriter, the truth can be a wounding exposé, but I suspect you'll find my clearing of the cobwebs a kind of purge. In return for this exclusive, I have a favor to ask."

I considered several options, then made a show of visibly relaxing through a minor shake-up in my disposition and by softening the angle of my posture.

"One day . . ." François began, when my current home at 118 rue de Turenne was still in progress and more an overture than a stack of lofts, he and my father had arranged to meet nearby at Café de Bretagne on an unelaborated business matter.

François had sipped two double espressos into chalk without a sighting of my father or an explanatory phone call. Having had the construction site pointed out to him on earlier occasions, François strolled there thinking my father might have been waylaid by some unexpected mishap.

The building's elevator shaft was still a silo, so François used the temporary, jungle gym–like stairs that climbed its veiled façade, searching each raw floor in turn, only to find solitary workers busy with the remodeling.

While wandering through these future rooms and former frameworks, he took note of their configurations. Each floor appeared to hold the sketch of two separate living quarters, one the anticipated loft and the other an extremely disadvantaged . . . apartment, perhaps, although François declared that term too grand, unless these adjunct dwellings' purpose was to let rats live like kings.

These smaller domiciles were no more imaginative than a hallway, lacking windows that could make them nest-like or any signs of doorways that might explain them as the guts of giant closets.

Upon reaching the building's highest floor, François overheard my father in discussion. Given that the words "secret passage" anchored every other sentence of the conversation, François said he'd crouched unseen until the strange domestic slivers were spelled out as means through which the lofts' inhabitants could be studied surreptitiously.

François then eased into my father's view. Accepting he'd been cornered, my father quickly sent the worker he'd been serenading on a mission to the nearest Starbucks.

The term "secret passage," he explained to François, was a kind of nickname, an inside joke for what would more prosaically constitute margins of error. Should one of his future tenants stiff him on the rent, he thought it might be helpful to have the means to discover certain faux pas—sequestered pets, drug paraphernalia, a secret mistress—that would give him legal recourse to occasion their eviction.

My father gave François a tour of these so-called margins, starting with their "headquarters," as he described it—a vast room that swilled the floor on which my father planned to live and whose only entrance would be a multitasking wall in his relatively trifling apartment.

In one corner of this room, a set of stairs no wider than the chutes on children's playground slides scraped and bumped them to a third-floor landing. There, one could either walk into that level's margin or descend into the second floor, and so on, until a secret exit on the ground floor could deposit one scot-free behind some trash cans in an alley.

Using one floor's half-built margin as a showcase, my father led François along its hall, explaining, between sidesteps of ladders and stops to dig the overhang of dangling wire tips from their hair, that the barren walls would fill with peepholes, each notch fitted with a fish-eye lens that would own a panoramic view of every corner of the corresponding loft.

Higher up, cameras would sit on metal perches, their minuscule lenses piercing the walls like mosquitos' stingers, draining imagery day and night from the lofts' defenseless rooms, then depositing their loot in the system's crowning headquarters.

To François, this seemed extravagant at best, and, at worst, a ghastly human zoo. Still, as he said I needn't be reminded, my father cloaked the explanation in his famous blaze airs and lulling, compound elocution such that François felt a probing question would have made him seem churlish.

A few weeks later, we had moved into the building, whereupon the objects of my father's lavish scrutiny became apparent. At a cocktail party held to christen the new homestead, François so poorly hid his feelings of betrayal that he was hurried from the other guests and taken into stricter confidence.

The secret world within the world was a necessity, my father told him, since Alfonse and I were "trouble" and "untrustworthy"—"lowlifes" prone to bartering his precious artworks for designer drug caches, "faux pastors" opening our lofts to every *jeune sans papiers* who shivered in the cardboard huts that spoiled Canal St. Martin's romantic banks.

François had seen enough of us to glean Alfonse's perfect manners and my utter selfishness. Hence, he found this newer lie even more impertinent, but . . . and here he paused briefly to dramatize the first of several bombshells . . . but . . . since his obsession with Alfonse had been a topic of my father's jokes for several years, he didn't feel he was positioned to find his friend's hyperbole distasteful.

From late that evening onward, my father phoned François nightly to share Alfonse's latest foibles. Fueled by François's rapt attention, he began to use the building's secret chambers as a means to do experiments, presumably to give his calls an even more addictive twist.

For example, Mon Petit Bichette had been awarded his position based not on any reassurance from his blatantly faked résumé, but rather on a law-abiding declaration that, prior to having found his current meds, he'd molested several adolescents, and, due to a side effect of this same medication, he didn't understand why that was such a problem.

Sure enough, within the space of days, my father claimed to have recordings of the nanny and my brother having sex on every horizontal surface and chairlike sculpture in their respective lofts that might cause tea bags not to seem surreal within the lens of François's glasses.

François envisioned screwing Alfonse in return for his discretion. At the very least, he'd hoped to share the building's secret vantage points, or, at the very, very least, be emailed torrents of the porn, but, as of yet, no perks had been granted him, nor did they seem to be imminent.

In fact, he might be masturbating in accordance with my father's every lurid word right now, he said, had the secret tests' success not inspired an even more ambitious form of interference. First, Mon Petit Bichette and Azmir were taught the marbled swarm's most ornamental tricks, then granted limited Svengali-like mastery over Alfonse and myself.

Thanks to their remote control, Alfonse and I had been revised over the course of several months from quirky siblings into a pair of unrequited, preening lovebirds.

A new file folder joined my brother's desktop. It fattened up with imagery wherein my face was Photoshopped into the rakish haircuts of his favorite mangas' heroes. This file had colonized his G4's hard drive into the useless, grinding hub of a peculiar slideshow that Alfonse would subjugate with X-rated whispers for hours at a stretch.

At first, I'd seemed resistant to my father's tampering, but, when the hidden cameras' zoom option was twirled, my jittering, impatient eyes were noticed circulating in my brother's pants, as though their creases were a complicated interchange.

I was faintly overheard exhaling "Alfonse" when I masturbated, and, more times than not, the name was lost in phrases and half sentences that signaled my imagination's need to murder him before it gave me satisfaction.

Azmir knew some tech-head, who was sneaked into my loft and who packed my browser's bookmarks with new links to sites for all variety of murderers whose specialties were children, assuming, presciently it seems, that I would welcome them too fondly to question how they had materialized.

When my clicks kept ringing up a German cannibal, related traps were set and sprung. For instance, a recent chat I'd undertaken on the biggest Klaus Freeh fansite, wherein I shared my dream to modify Alfonse into a mouthful, was not the private free-for-all I hoped, but instead an inquisition with my father playing dumb at the helm.

Here, I think it was, François confessed that while his schemes involving Alfonse had always ended badly and abruptly, their fatalities had been a practical decision since he'd learned by trial and error that, although his fetish life was rich, he had a problem with imprisonment.

The revolutionary thought that a postcoital Alfonse needn't feed some far-flung trash can or sewer grate, but, rather, be reborn as Alfonse Volume Two, had changed my living, breathing brother from the contraband of François's fantasies into a hindrance to his lauded culinary skills as well.

Accordingly, he had bargained with his sons, trading time-outs in their nightly molestations for an agreement to habituate Alfonse's favorite chat rooms and encourage him to drag me to this fair, where François had bribed officials then thrown up the off-the-record "booth" in which Alfonse was now a happy Flatso and unwitting prisoner.

With that, François said he'd altered quite enough of my reality for now and, after apologizing for any loose or hurried details that might have crimped his summary, he offered me a moment to inure myself before calling in the reimbursive favor.

You who've read this far with any care and feel you know me to the point to which you've been empowered will have gleaned what I would like you to assume I felt when told my recent life had been the colophon of someone else's trail of bread crumbs.

Despite the face of reason I'm reasonably certain I maintained throughout, the full-fledged me to whom you've been tangentially invited had weathered my initial disbelief, then more or less evolved into someone who felt weird about my outbursts as an air guitarist and regretted certain times and ways I'd cheered on my ejaculates, but who was far more flattered by such exorbitant attention.

Perhaps you've noted my disinterest in relaying stories from my sex life apart from claiming to have had something of one. It's not simply that I find the terms of sex to be at odds with my decorum, although there's that excuse. Nor can blame be placed entirely on my need to squelch your zeal to find me gay as charged if colored by some version of psychosis. But since we're just about to undertake my story's first lascivious scene, perhaps it's time to touch up my image.

If it truly were as simple as my being gay but undermined, I would repeat one of the standard faux apologies I always seem to make to those for whom my listless, nerve-wracked body proves so disenchanting. Well, I'll tell you nonetheless because I suppose that's how I am.

What I'm into, in quotes, and the one arrangement that, say, were I to be hit on in a public setting, might find me snuggled in the backseat of a taxi, would be if, using me as bait, this suitor were to lure another party into ours, where-upon, after forming a trio on whatever mattress proved convenient, said couple were to fuck in some eye-pleasing manner while I, naked if absolutely necessary and posed nearby, fulfill a sidekick role, perhaps akin to the porn DVD unwheeling in the corner of the eye of some drunk straight guy who lets a gay acquaintance masturbate him with his mouth.

In other words, I'm into three-ways, and, more precisely, into gang fucks, in the vaguest terms imaginable, or, more ide-ally, being studied by two worshippers who take a dip into my privates on occasion to . . . I believe the term is "service" me with oral and tactile stimulation and perhaps some verbalized incentives befitting my enticements—for instance, gentle barks to spread my legs.

I see this setup as a form of self-prevention since I am thereby restricted in what I can achieve within the sex at hand by my concern that what I do and say not disappoint those who are relying on my surface.

Yes, my special needs can make it difficult to score, and no one ever ends up thanking God for meeting me, but I am comfortable there.

By all rights, given the eurhythmy of my face, I should rightly be what gay guys call a bottom, a recipient, the intersected, a passive partner, yet whenever I attempted to accept what seemed to be my fate in this regard back in my early teens, I cried uncontrollably and felt I couldn't breathe, not from any pelting ache in my invaded nether reaches, if you're wondering, and in fact I . . . well, you'll see for yourselves once or if I have the nerve or guts to call back those disasters.

If I seem prone to introspection as it is, you should be thrilled I'm not dictating or rather whining and sobbing out this saga in your bed, and I assure you those who'd hoped to fuck a static, deaf-mute version of my body would rise from their graves to attest.

Those who are clinically depressed—and Serge, if you remember him, would be a prime example—can sometimes reach a tolerable zombie-like state thanks to a fine-tuned mix and match of prescription medications.

For me, getting laid has always been a similarly trial-and-error fête, albeit with naked males in place of pills.

I only mention this to explicate more fully why having been spied upon and toyed with by my father didn't outrage me or cause me to feel vengeful in the slightest. Rather, it inspired a most intensive curiosity as to his motivation.

I had coveted life as a movie idol in my adolescence, and, after wrecking several acting classes, I was made more than aware that were I to pursue acting as my livelihood, I would expect to have a brief, forgettable career playing snarky teenaged loudmouths who leech their girlfriends off more central characters.

Thus, I might have viewed my father as an over-weening stage parent and my part in François's plot against my brother as the kind of juicy, long-awaited role for which my limited propensities were made—an end result I still believe since, forced or not, it means I hadn't been in love with him when they'd miscast me as his suitor.

Nonetheless, in case I'm wrong, and if I haven't pointed out too many secrets in this tale to busy you already, you might watch out for yet another sidetrack, this one shapeless like the underhanded moonlighting of love itself and sneaking underneath the favor I was thrilled if wildly unprepared to grant.

I will exclude our more or less half-hour drive through the relatively pricey fifteenth arrondissement of Paris because to re-create its vistas would exhaust an afternoon that could have spun effectively enough in a few explosive sentences.

If you seek the crux behind the grinding tack I've used throughout this story, I'll need to conjugate the so-called marbled swarm my voice has long since adopted with an asterisk from my father's.

As briefly as possible, and rather like a magician requesting a coin or handkerchief from a member of his audience, I'll ask for a wad of your imagination.

Let's say the room where you are reading this is like the vestibules that interlace my story. In other words, it's side-swiped by a hidden room or passage. Let's also say, for convenience sake, this secret room conjoins the very wall you're facing at the moment.

If you're reading this when on the metro or while soaking in the lamblike nature of a park, we have an issue. In that case, you might divide us with a bookmark, head home, and then rejoin me in your bedroom, although any indoor spot whose walls are dulled by inattentiveness will work.

Once you're reoriented there and have checked out the dividing line I've just impugned, if only to amuse yourself, prepare for what will constitute a shock.

Contrary to the bio note that tags this volume's jacket or downloaded file, I'm not, in truth, oh, dead or lengthily imprisoned, to take a guess. Instead, I'm still at large and writing this while closeted behind the very wall at which you peer so trustingly, my right eye watching through a peephole, using your absorbed or wearied or excited face as my narrative's adjusting guideline.

In other words, everything you've read thus far was gauged to vex, engage, bore, amuse you, and so forth precisely as it has done. That's to say, using prose only slightly fancier than that to which you are accustomed, I've reduced the "you" who'd hoped to crack some risqué memoir into my marbled swarm's by-product. Like father like son, essentially.

Point is, should you stubbornly continue to believe this memoir's point and only worth lies in delineating Serge's gruesome death or treasure hunting the chateau or solving Jean-Paul's dangling riddle, and so on—in other words, rescuing that story from the background that has swamped it—you might have logic on your side and the odds in your favor, but I'll remind you of how ill-advised my life had been until François's tattletale unstuck my dumbstruck eyes.

Had I decided as my life's official author that the goal was supervising the exploits and porn my recent time on earth has technically entailed, you might turn my final page more tickled or grossed out than would seem to be your destiny, but you would also leave here double-crossed.

All that said, I'm also stalling at the moment since the greatest weakness of my tossed-together marbled swarm is that, when I'm aroused, this highfalutin mush I call a voice melts in my mouth, and as much as I'm okay with barking like a dog to some degree, I know I sound stupid when I do.

But I believe I've made that point extremely clear in much the same words previously if not repeatedly, which speaks yet again to my nervousness.

Perhaps I'll use the convenient grayness of our drive to introduce Olivier, François's quote-unquote elder son, whose dash of an appearance here in Slat's role has left him barely creased within a scene where his realities will factor.

At the moment, Olivier and Alfonse are sandwiched inside Slat and Plank, and they are wedged into the car's backseat like surfboards.

François, myself, and Log are in the front seat. I'll also add that the arousal I just referenced is, if not contingent on my seatmate then sharpened by its handiwork, which has been vested in my lap since François hit the gas, and is now, as best I can surmise, trying to unite Log's crotch and mine as if they were the handles of a sliding door.

So, Olivier was initially the offspring of a housekeeper from Tokyo who'd worked for François years before. Kenji was his given name. When she perished in a traffic accident, not a relative or friend offered condolences, much less claimed the child, so Kenji just kept living under François's roof by proxy.

When enrolling Olivier in school required a parent's signature, François renamed the boy, then put his scrawl above the dotted line. Still, for all intents and purposes, Olivier is just a false report or stage-named shape in which a missing, now forgotten boy has been declared unborn.

Now, returning you to François's car, a Peugeot Pullman Turbo, for the record, we'd just left the smooth-ish sailing of the Quai d'Orsay for a tony neighborhood wherein the only thing I knew was that François's home would cordon off the favor I've neglected to define for you, I'm sorry.

The street was disconcertingly familiar, as was each café,

boulangerie, and every cross street where we turned too sharply for my taste.

Had I opted to describe our drive, the adjectives with which I clarified this phase would decorate an anecdote about the days when childhood mischief let me use the bushes we were speeding past to urinate or hide and smoke a cigarette.

Anyway, it wasn't shocking when the residence where François parked—a Haussmann-style mansion whose coveted location on the Champs de Mars put its value in the 12-to-14-million-euro range—was in fact our house, or, rather, the home from which my broken family had moved just months before.

One could excuse this weird coincidence as François having bought the grievous building off my father's hands and hoping to surprise Alfonse and me. Since truth is, of course, a technicality, this is in fact the explanation, but let me add that there is far more to the symbiosis, and that I may even tell you.

Slat was lugged out of the car and steadied on its feet, then it and Log swayed and dashed respectively into the mansion's nearest bathroom, presumably to scrub away the Flatso makeup, which they had started scratching with impunity.

François amused himself by giving Plank and me a tour of the house that would have proved jejune were not the rooms so dandified that their familiar shells and measurements had the airiness of déjà vus.

The white, art-friendly walls favored to the point of obsolescence by my father had been filtered out with breezily historic wallpaper that made our old home look as though it had been gift wrapped at the Musée des arts et métier.

The polished wooden floors on which my stocking feet had pedaled like a frightened cartoon hare's were secluded under rugs that looked like giant grassy playing cards—that is, when you could even see the rugs through all the antique chairs and tables.

As much as I had bitched about the chrome and glass and steel objects whose tart edges would slice and bruise my wilder, younger legs, at least those fixtures knew which century they were decorating.

Thankfully, the tour was curtailed due to the special needs mandated by my brother's Flatso incarnation. For, despite the costume's magical conceits of flight and presto-change-o travel, its nuts and bolts disabled him, making every doorway a combatant and the staircase as forbidding as a rope thrown off a cliff top.

Our route dead-ended in what François called the master bedroom. As I have no reason to suspect he didn't sleep there and fill its chests with his belongings, I'll retain his definition.

Still, in every other way, it was Alfonse's former bedroom, exactly as he'd left it, which would have been incredibly unnerving even if the same decor had not been boxed up, trucked, unpacked, and reconstructed in his loft.

Alfonse had lined the walls with animation cells secreted from his favorite anime, most of them acquired through flighty bids at online auctions. In their places, hanging from the same nails, I imagine, François had framed and hung convincing forgeries and high-grade scans of art book reproductions.

A custom-made Tezuka dresser proved impossible to duplicate, François explained. So, to establish his devotion, he'd paid some Chinese artisan to carve a replica from balsa wood, and he raised the sculpture halfway to the ceiling on a crooked baby finger to demonstrate its uselessness.

Three lamps, still dangling IKEA tags, were arranged strategically around the room. The bulbs were burning at their brightest, and the shades were trained directly at a copy of my brother's futon, blasting it into a stage while so neglecting the room's outskirts they formed a darkened auditorium.

So impressive or psychotic was this cyclorama, it took Plank's expert eye to spot some unconnected items—sex toys, lube, a towel, in a nutshell—that occupied Alfonse's "bedside table," which, had it been granted authenticity, would have held an Asterix alarm clock and a glass of water, if memory serves.

It was the first of many times when François's cock-rock bent wreaked hell with my oblique approach, and I wasn't saddened in the slightest when, after wishing us a pleasant birthday, he stepped so far into the bedroom's unlit sticks I could pretend he'd left the room entirely if he hadn't.

Plank had been unusually—or, given that I didn't know Plank, characteristically—amped throughout the tour, grabbing everything François identified as priceless and, in its screechy voice, which I'll describe as Mickey Mouse without the stuffed nose, declaring each trinket something it could use or couldn't in its home dimension.

Now, Plank stood gravely at the bedside table handling the sex toys, its opinions lost to me within the Flatso makeup that had whitewashed and paralyzed my brother's normally outgoing face.

"Where I live," Plank said, "things such as these, while no doubt necessary, are inferred rather than depicted, sort of like the nails and screws that keep the homes in this dimension upright."

"Has my admittedly roundabout behavior these past few months so masked the squalor I've been nursing in your presence that its evidence perplexes you," I asked.

Plank exhaled loudly through its nose, although let me reiterate how Flatsos seemed not so much to breathe as use their mouths and nostrils to disturb the air like birds' wings.

"My true fear was that you would never cease talking," Plank said. "In my world, speech, and thought itself perhaps, are annotated into gasps and grrs and wows except in cases of emergency."

"I don't understand this kind of love," I said. "I'm speaking of the sort wherein the offer of one's body is encoded with a handshake of agreement that its content is legitimate."

"Again, in my world," Plank said, "the exchange of which you speak is not confusing in the slightest. In fact, we frequently shake hands, as you put it, without any prior agreement whatsoever."

"Even when the advocates are brothers," I asked.

"Only in a sense," Plank said. "Due to the interchangeable faces we've been given, we're less brothers by the definition you address than clones sporting very slight mistakes. We certainly have sex, and more continually than we walk, and yet our world itself is very chaste, almost as taintless as your Disney films, which explains why we wear blurs beneath our underwear, if you've ever wondered."

"Are these clones in love when they . . . intersect," I asked.

"On your conditions, I suppose," Plank said. "Still, if one desires someone or something that, barring a minutely different hair color, is yourself in quotes, is it love that causes one to wish to share their bed or a display of confidence?"

"Our being brothers should preclude the need to tie the knot, in theory," I said, "but our case is rather special, you'll agree, given that we've synchronized ourselves like showgirls, and perhaps it's this coherence that inspires my need to grasp you as completely as I know myself."

With that, I groped the swatch of costume where my brother's ass would then have squished between my fingers were he dressed in jeans or naked.

I rubbed the cardboard slowly in a circle, which, additionally to having no effect on my intended target, was embarrassing and made a boring, scratchy noise.

"I will tell Alfonse you've done the unimaginable," Plank said.

Pretending to have spotted something glinty on the floor, I crouched and fiddled briefly with the phantom jewel or coin, then, gambling my precious touch would trump the doofish pose that might result, I tagged the stretch of naked calf that Plank's short, rigid skirt had left exposed.

I clutched the leg to stay on board, whereupon its warmth, which was quickly raised to blistering in my imagination, seemed to acculturate the room into a kitchen and me into an idiot to whom I'll now relent for the sake of accuracy.

"I would snap away this leg as violently as one unbinds a chicken's drumstick," I said, "then chew and swallow until bone halted my teeth if I could thereby know you."

"Being that my goal is to forget the silly nerd who's wearing me," Plank said, "you're welcome to him, but I fear I cannot help you."

Plank raised its human hands and studied them, not so much confusedly as in a funk, as far as I could tell, perhaps like werewolves eye the flimsy thumbs wherein their godlike claws have just retracted. Then it grabbed the towel and started freeing Alfonse's visage from its make-up, forehead first.

"I want to know what Mon Petit Bichette already knows," I said.

I shoved one hand in Plank's internal organs then climbed Alfonse's thighs, my forearm knocking like the clapper in a fissured bell, until my knuckles brushed the frilling of his genitals, which, like mistletoe, seemed far too folksy to award me so much latitude.

"He doesn't know very much," said Alfonse's usual if slightly muffled voice. "Why, what did that creep say?"

"I find myself wondering," I said, "if there are manga lovers like yourself whose fondest wish is not to wind up thin enough to mark a book but rather torn or hacked into pieces small enough to slide down someone's throat."

Alfonse peeked at me above the blotchy towel. His looks had reconnected with their faculties and basic shapes, and Plank's poker face was largely an unhealthy color. "You're speaking of Guro," he said. "An interesting subgenre, though a bit macho for me."

"Do these Guro lovers fraternize with your more genial contingent," I asked.

"We do socialize, or, rather, their avatars have been known to sneak within our sites without detection," he said. "However, their foul mouths cause them to be blocked in almost every case."

"It must so frustrate them, and you as well, to undertake such absolutist missions," I said. "Consider this painstaking mock-up of your bedroom, which so clearly forms a homonym for François's useless dream of sharing it with you."

I should mention that, by then, I'd started masturbating Alfonse, which, given the costume's bottlenecking, was surely more impressive as a juggling act.

"Perhaps you feel as I do that birthdays come with certain privileges," Alfonse said. "The truth is sex, although that term seems so uncivil, intrigues me. When I've been given any say, I always ask my . . . partners, as you call them, to rest on top of me. Since they've weighed far more than I thus far, there is the side effect of feeling squished, which you know I rather covet.

"For that reason, I see beds, or floors, assuming they are clean, as the earthly likenesses of manga pages in which I'm merely ink or pixels and my partner is a rather heavy-handed draughtsman. Plus, the more unreal I've found myself, the better the . . . sex has been for everyone involved, if, that is, I even vaguely understand what gets men off, which is to say François is cleared to join us, should you agree."

"My issue with sex," I said, "or the first of many—and I too speak that catchword grudgingly—is the transience of its effect. To think that afterward, you'll reinflate, and I will only have crossed incest off a wish list I hadn't yet compiled. If only you, no, we could stay, oh, razor-thin in your case and unrealistically wild-mannered in mine."

"Clearly, if I could stay unreal with any permanence, I would," he said. "I haven't imitated you for years because I find your affects therapeutic."

With that, he started patting down the Flatso costume's image of a shirt and scratching at its painted buttons. Seeing his futility, I freed my arm, then, gripping the "shirt's" collar, tried to rip Plank into shreds.

"You didn't keep a pair of scissors handy that François might have reproduced," I asked.

It was then the words "Velcro straps," spoken with a lechery that neither one of us had any feel for, broke into our conversation.

Of course, the speaker was François, who, quite naturally, had been lurking in the dark, but perhaps because my eyes were so bedazzled by our spotlights, his voice seemed less substantial than the sawing of a cricket's legs.

There is in fact another explanation for its wisp, but I will let you discover it, if you do, at the same time and manner as I did, if I ever fully have.

Once the Velcro bindings were unlocked, the costume sledded up and past my brother's head with only the subtlest misplacing of his hair.

I sought an unobtrusive spot to dump the Flatso's corpse, ultimately leaning it against a wall. By the time I turned my full attention to Alfonse, he'd lain facedown upon the futon and struck a pose that seemed designed to make him feel, if not quite look, as scarce as possible.

His body could have been a jar, figurative and dyed one of the paler human colors—his name a label steamed then peeled away, so poorly did it warn me not to take his status as my brother lightly.

"Are you as specious as you appear," I asked. "Because even using the familiar form of 'you' just felt like guesswork."

"Just before the act of sex commences, I feel an agonizing realness," Alfonse said. "While this pose has been the most effective of my tryouts, there is a minor defect—namely, my penis winds up pressed against the bed, which stimulates it by default. Fortunately, the pain of being . . . and I hate this word too, 'fucked,' tends to draw the bigger picture."

"If we're to speak so openly of defects," I said, "I'll admit to one that seems germane. Like you, I'm gorgeous, you'll admit, and, accustomed as I am to being hit upon, I've felt no need to learn assailants' social skills. In other words, I need a minute."

I sat along the futon's edge, then eyed my brother as a mountain climber might assess a model of the Pyrenees. As I replayed the porn whose choreography was well adapted to my halting bedside manner, I fiddled with Alfonse's ass as though its fat and muscle were the pivoting components of a Rubik's Cube.

I'd never slept with such a pip-squeak, and any child porn I'll admit to having viewed was so antiquely filmed its stars were only boys the way Seurat's arrays of dots are women. Nonetheless, it didn't seem bizarre that, having dreamt Alfonse would sport an asshole as understated as the rest of him, I was stunned to find a wound so serious it would have killed him had the harm not been so evidently reckoned into place.

Later, under François's tutelage, I would learn to tell the building blocks of pricey entrées from the chaff that goes in dog bowls, but in my innocence that afternoon, having struck a vein of what was sitting in my fridge was more important than the clues that made it fool's gold.

"Perhaps Alfonse would like to listen to some music," said François's voice.

I retrieved my brother's backpack from the floor and rummaged through its mishmash until I'd clutched the cold hard outlines of an iPod.

"What do manga characters listen to when they're . . . ?" I asked him.

"Nothing, strangely," Alfonse said. "I think because the sound of music proves difficult to draw. It's true that, in addition to their superhero duties, they often moonlight as a boy band, yet when these bands are shown performing, the only way we know they're not delivering a lecture is because their open mouths shoot lightning bolts. But I wouldn't mind hearing *Cartoon KAT-TUN II You*."

As I've more than hinted at so often, I'm undone by the formalities of having sex. And yet, from all reports, I seem no less engaged than were I watching someone rob a store across my street while chronicling the bandit's moves over the phone.

Perhaps this politesse is an affliction of the marbled swarm itself, because the same capacity to disengage from goings-on, no matter how logistically involving or oppressive, bewitched my father too, if I may jump this story's gun for just a second.

A few weeks after the event I'm reimagining, my father's shoe skewered a pockmark in the floor of what, to that point, I'd understood to be the central office of our building's enterprise of secret chambers, causing him to trip and strike his head, and rather fiercely if a ragged trail of blood was any indication.

He returned to his apartment as if nothing had occurred. So confident was he that the bleeding would be squelched by tissues and some elbow grease, he didn't close the secret door behind him, leaving the hidden loft exposed, and I will speak of the renaissance this lack of foresight occasioned in my life a little later.

We know he made some notes and phone calls until, gonged by a headache, he reclined upon a couch, hoping to undo it with a nap, which amplified into a coma in which Azmir, reporting back from some nefarious assignment, discovered him.

A siren's endless bleating finally coaxed me to a window of my loft, where I observed my slack-jawed father being rolled inside an ambulance, which sped to Hospital St. Louis, where he then lived in quotes for days but never woke, or not according to the terms by which that word is most employed.

Let's say I'd tripped, albeit mentally and only vis-à-vis my hand, and my fingertips dead-ended in Alfonse's crotch, resting on that archway's penile frill no longer than my father's head had touched the floorboards' wood grain, which caused me to cease thinking by my standards, even if my recollection of those thoughts seemed typically too decorative to you.

While his stiffened penis was, of course, the compliment I'd sought, the general conditions, specifically the humid airspace hard-ons always author, unnerved me, perhaps the way a sick child's forehead curls his mother's fingers.

So, even as I basked, I was inveigled by a mood of hopelessness that, in retrospect, has proved to be more advantageous than a drag, I suppose.

It was as if I'd found a light switch in a room too dark to navigate or leave, the unit's surface strangely heated by a recent short along its hidden wiring, the switch already raised into the "on" position.

I will barely be speaking for a while. I might begin to seem a child who mouths the roars and motor revvings of his toys. Or I might grunt with satisfaction now and then like a lowly member of some demolition crew in action.

I stepped out of my shoes, scrolled down my socks, unbuttoned my shirt, lowered my pants and underwear, then threw and slid myself away from all of them.

François was talking on his cell phone or, more precisely, saying a "Yes" or "I'm still here," when, that is, his voice was not too muffled by my brother's ass, which he had leveled with his fingers and was sniffing like a messy line of very good cocaine.

"Does this look strange," he asked, having noticed something in my face I had not placed there to address something about him.

I responded that to see a man of his renown treating Alfonse as far more renowned was interesting, but if my face seemed like the outlay of some burgeoning critique, he was likely overthinking me.

I believe it was then that I wound up lying on the bed by some means I don't recall.

Had what occurred been filmed, it might have looked less namby-pamby than the fans of child pornography prefer, but, judging by the bits I've watched, our merge of young and old and cute and gross fell well along those troubling lines.

To wit, a boy lay stiffly on a bed, looking X-ray–like without his clothes, his face stricken, often frowny, but uncomplaining, his body game enough despite a shyness that clenched his joints into a mannequin's.

A less illegal teenager, demoted to a sidekick by his co-star's shocking scale, lay nearby, acting as a fluffer, if, that is, patting the boy's head and shoulders qualifies, and otherwise so snubbed by everyone around him that his body might have been imprinted on the bedding.

Meanwhile, an older man no more suited to the task of heating porn than the adolescent played the uninvited guest whose love of fucking little boys gives kiddie porn its dubious je ne sais quoi and brings the rare intellectual to its defense.

In the commotion, first one earphone then the other jiggled from Alfonse's head. They writhed across the rocky bed until the iPod bounced onto the floor with such a thwack that I could tell the thing was broken without reclaiming it.

I only mention this because the wilder sound of François's panting and my occasional asides didn't bring my brother back to life, by which I mean revive the squeaking, flopping figurine into a boy who might have asked for a time-out.

I barely saw my brother's thinking in his eyes, and based on how they skirted me, I felt I wasn't needed anymore. When he did talk, repeating "nos" and "don'ts" I might not even mention, the orders either weren't for me or I'd stopped listening like a brother.

At some stage, one of us, most likely me, wanted to fetch a block of kitchen knives, thinking we could hack Alfonse out of our way then strip his undergrowth and gulp it down like monkeys—that is, if primates even eat like that outside cartoons.

The other one of us, clearly François on second thought, cautioned me that acting like wild animals hadn't leant us their capacities, and that we still had nubs for teeth and quibbling digestive tracks.

He described the meal Alfonse could yield if I were patient, reinventing every sweaty inch of flesh at which my finger aimed into a knickknack that would stun the patrons of L'Alstrance, and, if properly refrigerated, more lengthily suspend an auctioneer than any object in my father's art collection.

Thus, I gradually lost sight of who'd been suited up inside Alfonse for twelve years of my life, and who could barely move his limbs or use his forehead as a place to scribble incoherently about his pains and worries.

His breaths were drafts, his whines and gripes the creaking

of his face, and his skull a lattice where some flesh had grown and taken on its human shape.

By the time I heard some knocks and scraping in the bedroom's darkened apron, and Azmir glowed into my view, watching François land upon and raise himself from someone's back had put my eyes on such a treadmill that seeing anything untoward was a relief.

Azmir looked vaguely familiar, period, and he mutinied with every dud he shed into the most unreasonably well-hung guy I'd ever seen outside my desktop. His penis warped and strained his underwear diaphanous, then walloped free and jousted with the air like an amputee's gesticulating stump until he stilled it with his hands.

Having watched dozens of asses, most no bigger than my brother's, grit their holes in hopes of safeguarding their owners' lives, the spectacle has lost its wow. Hence, I lack the naivete to brief you on Alfonse's turn, so he will have to fend within the action sequence I'll recount.

Azmir rolled my brother over like a herpetologist upends a rock to search for napping snakes, then pinched his penis, which François had long since milked and wrung into a whisker, and used a fingertip to twirl his testicles into a tiny turban.

He threw my brother's legs out of his way, then clawed the ass as if it were a bush that hid another unsuspecting creature, perhaps a scorpion or something of that general nastiness.

Azmir's penis pinned my brother's asshole to his deepest pelvic bones, then, it seemed to me, tried to erase it like a stray pencil mark.

He scrubbed the stain until the ass itself appeared to change metabolisms—wilting, liquefying, and sloshing up against my brother's skeleton before it finally jelled and shrink-wrapped what was basically a crater.

Azmir erased the hole until the ass itself became un-hinged, halving like the trap door in a gallows, whereupon his cock inched slowly underground and Alfonse's feeble tissues made the pops and crackling noises of a campfire.

Azmir raped my brother for an hour-long few minutes. When the cock was airborne, it was heavily upholstered, and when it slugged inside, Alfonse's blood would spritz Azmir's thighs and glug onto the bed, which was rapidly discolored.

Alfonse began to watch something, what, I'm not entirely certain. It seemed to fly in circles, and to not be of this earth, or so I gathered since he'd never looked that horrified by any-thing before.

Suddenly, whatever had compiled Alfonse's skull and skin and cartilage into a face stopped working, but I thought he looked incredible. I thought if he had always looked that un-demonstrative, he would have been famous, although I had no idea for what reason.

François seemed content to watch my brother blanch and crystallize into a less involving boy and nonspecific shape, but I felt strangely unprepared for that divide.

Once Alfonse and I had played a game of Truth or Dare, if you remember, in which I'd introduced his death throes as a form of entertainment. When given every option to expire, Alfonse had not picked being fucked to death or any other fate that was another word for blood loss. Instead, he'd opted to be steamrolled, and, when this memory returned to me, I argued that his wish be granted, although I guess I thought we'd use a car.

I was too adamant to follow François's logic that, since "Alfonse" was now a body's dying title, we could no more grant his wish than kissing Oscar Wilde's grave marker while wearing lipstick can retract the author's loneliness.

I recall our hobbling down a staircase more than how I talked us into being there. Azmir held my brother upside down, and I trotted alongside, and François twitched a cut-glass bowl half full of nougats underneath Alfonse's head in hopes of catching blood before it scabbed his carpet.

After a treacherous right turn that left us standing in a pool of candies, and a traffic jam while François solved a dead bolt, we found ourselves in the garage, which seemed unaltered since my mother had scarcely used it as the place where guests could smoke when it was raining.

Azmir explained how gore behaved, such as its tendency to use young, flimsy stomachs as fire exits and redeploy the eyes, nostrils, and mouth as launching pads for its projectiles, whereupon it was agreed the body should be laid facedown upon the concrete floor.

In one corner of the room, there was a hefty wooden can that looked to have been fished from movie pirate waters. It was three-quarters full of very dark, wet dirt, having been filled by François's gardener as he revamped a flower bed in the mansion's small front yard the afternoon before.

The can was leaden, but, between the three of us, we yanked it airborne then rocked and scraped the bottom six or seven steps to where Alfonse reclined, using his last few brain cells to inflate and slump his upper back.

As the only light source was a glary ceiling lamp, the can gave off an oblong shadow that became an evil spotlight. When my brother's feet were charcoaled, François counted down from five, and we let go.

While I would love to say we left an animation cell depicting dainty feet, I will say we left him socks engorged with children's cheapest Christmas gifts, and even that peculiar image does Alfonse's last impression quite a favor.

We moved the spotlight, smashing circle after circle flat as best we could. His knees and thighs took seven drops to look like baggy legs. The sculpture garden in his hips was chipped away and finally buckled, although not into the mush I'd hoped, and only after Azmir climbed atop the can and stomped the final centimeter.

Between our weariness and percolating sweat, which caused the can to roam within our hands—and I'll admit my lifts were something of an act, and the can a portly Ouija board—it took eight drops before the upper torso was a mat.

The shoulders never lost their crossbar look, and even hacking it out of their initial barbell took forever.

My brother's head had no resolve but went down shooting—eyeballs, teeth, tongue, and very abstract objects coughed out of his cavities and nostrils, or would bash themselves new shortcuts where needed.

Every time we raised the can, his mouth was more outstretched, until it dwarfed his face as much as any alligator's.

I couldn't think, and even that insouciance was canceled out when every dead celebrity whose surreptitious morgue shot I had Googled massed against me from the far ends of my memory and snapped their fingers in my face.

I must have sobbed since even Azmir asked if I was still myself, albeit with the leeriness that stars of movies check on costars who've been chewed upon by zombies.

The garage had a second door so hidden by a stack of cardboard boxes in my family's tenure that, until François turned its knob, I'd always thought it had been stored against the wall just like the cargo piled in front of it.

It led onto a brick footpath that gentrified a tight-knit residue of space between the mansion's southern wall and neighbor's fence, where François used a garden hose to wash the blood and splatter off our legs.

I was put in charge of fetching our respective outfits from the master bedroom, and, therewith, pardoned from the manly task awaiting François and Azmir—namely, shoveling the afterimage of my brother off the floor and into some container.

As I think I've mentioned, I no more spend time reading novels than you would kill your brothers. Hence, how authors give dead characters' survivors room to grieve while, presumably within the same handful of paragraphs, checking off new plot twists as though nothing diabolical has happened is wizardry to me.

Still, I know enough to guess that, having not just killed Alfonse but sort of cried, I should be out of kilter, so I'll try to wreck the next few pages of my story in some self-effacing fashion, and, thus, this decimation has begun, not that you or even I could swear to it.

Scaling the death row through which my brother had been hurried, and not so many months after it had formed a bumpy slide down which he would repeatedly kerplunk and laugh astride a giant piece of cardboard, proved a more disorienting hike than the incline had portended.

I'd reached the first-floor landing and laid my hand upon the banister, when I heard a throat clear to my left, whereupon a voice sourced from the same distinctive set of vocal chords asked, "What happened in there."

Peering down the hallway, I saw an Asian boy with waist-length hair—a coiffure christened "Gloomy Girl" when it was fashionable, meaning two years prior for several months. It was purportedly inspired by the hairstyle of the daughter in Pixar's *The Incredibles*, i.e., a dour teen whom I believe could turn invisible, if that helps you imagine him.

He was shirtless and barefoot, wearing the fattened, low-slung jeans that young suburbanites procure from fake designer clothing stores around Les Halles, then, as if mystically possessed by the street cred of their style's hip-hop progenitors, they begin to speak in syncopated rhymes to their disapproving parents.

Let me add that, as in the cases of Azmir and Didier, this boy's speaking patterns are too explosive for my idiom, and I will make him sound as though he sounds vaguely like me but with an edge.

As bleary as the post-Alfonse world looked to me, I guessed he was Olivier, François's sort of son. Still, even accounting for the politesse I lazily associate with everyone Eurasian, his vibe seemed too blase given I was naked and had not yet lost the bulk of my erection.

"Exactly what I'm sure it sounded like," I said evenly.

"Are you finished," he asked, again without a trace of curiosity.

He was leaning gently to the right, one hand splayed and resting on a wall, but not as lightly as his tilt would warrant. The palm was tensed into a Gothic arch, the fingers flexing on their whitened tips. Meanwhile, his other hand, which I'd misread as settled in a pocket, was rumpling his flabby jeans and tending an erection that seemed no less out of place than mine.

"Granted, it doesn't feel like we're finished, but logic says we are," I said.

"So, does this mean you're going home," he asked.

"Your father thinks my leaving is appropriate, and it's not for me to disagree," I said.

"Were you to stall for just a minute, I think you would be interested by what's in there," he said, eyeing the wall his hand was scrunching. "By that I don't mean Didier, although you'll likely find him interesting as well, or, as 'interest' might be pushing it, useful, since, as I'm confident my father told you, he's a prodigy regarding other people's penises, and you clearly seem to have one.

"All I ask as recompense is that you consider me the vague

beginnings of a friend. Truth is, while a life of tragedies and sexual abuse has hollowed me into a disbeliever in the scuttlebutt concerning love, there is, in addition to your total foxiness, a lack of something or other about your personage that I find sympathetic."

"You seem to know some of my passwords," I said carefully. "Still, as I rank a change of scenery at the top of my priorities, and since I've spent a billion seconds of my life strolling idly past the stretch of wall you speak of so mysteriously, it will need something more magnetic than your proximity and implications."

"Well," he replied, "let me ask you how, while I was evidently not with you in our garage, I could nonetheless describe its recent occupation in disturbing, graphic detail, and then explain why my erection, which I'm confident you've noted, would not have lost a centimeter, and thereby press my point that we're of likened minds."

"It's true that I am rarely this susceptible," I said, "and yet, as you seem set to verify, I just murdered my own brother. Far worse, or even stranger at the very least, I'm neither having second thoughts nor do I feel I've finished anything of real importance—a lack of loyalty that has inspired its own insidious brand of horror, I assure you.

"What I'm sorting through behind these words, should you be curious, is how killing him involved a problem that I

also have with, say, the Nouvelle Vague—i.e., supposed classic films that seem to spellbind everyone with any brains but
me—meaning the murder lacked a high point or dramatic
arc where I could tell myself, 'It's now or never,' and, frankly,
masturbate the scene into an aftermath.

"Maybe that point was when he died, but it was difficult
to know exactly when he did, and the violence was so frontal
and his heartbeat such a needle in the haystack that I didn't
seem to care that we spent half the time redesigning a cadaver,
much less my brother's.

"Thus, while I wouldn't mind—peculiarly, if you know
me—giving Didier a whirl and then comparing notes on our
respective disassociations, I'm also like a child who's just de-
barked a carousel and feels himself still spinning, even though
he's in the line to ride a roller coaster."

Surmising, correctly I suppose, that my wending self-
incrimination was a fulsome way of saying "yes," Olivier
ceased his finger exercises, skittering the hand across the wall
until it found a filthy bit of otherwise well-tidied molding.

He pinched the grunge, whereupon the wall itself
swung open, not stormily enough to fill the hall with
bursting splinters or rip his arm out of its socket, and just
as handily as if it were a hinged door, which, after Didier
had bolted from what looked at first to be a hidden closet,
I ascertained it was.

Didier was nothing much to look at, but his face had possibilities. Think of Leonardo DiCaprio, post-*Titanic*, and, more specifically, of his head's vast sweeps and curves of unused skin in which his features seem to gang up like the finger holes in a bowling ball. Now drizzle that with Kurt Cobain's scraggly hair at its most unwashed, and you will sort of have the crux of Didier's outstanding issues at your fingertips.

In other words, he wasn't quite the eyesore François claimed, but—and here I'll test out my ill-fitting gaydar for a moment—more a kind of fixer-upper—or, speaking from the future as a hardened cannibal—well, you know how, when you're stripping someone you're about to fuck, the first thing you abscond with is his shoes? When one prefers to eat a boy than sleep with him, his face is like that.

So, while I was no more tantalized by him than little girls holding baby dolls are mothers, it seems my wish to leave the house in which Alfonse was so exceptionally imprinted and furiously carved, meaning in everything and everyone, myself included, encouraged me to crowd inside the strange new door with Didier, then walk and crouch and finally crawl behind him down a wooden cave, or so I thought, squeezed and burrowed through unceasing treasuries of spiderwebs and insulation that slowly rubbed the home into the ghost of any structure I had entered in my life, until we found the world's most secret exit, and I used it.

F ive weeks after someone in the Paris art world bribed my father's dust into a ritzy plot in Cemetery Montparnasse that had been held for Liliane Bettencourt before her scandals, his lawyer sent me a strangely exuberant if technically proficient email suggesting we meet that afternoon and parse the estate I was destined to inherit.

My father hadn't changed his will to suit my brother's absence, and, in any case, its spillage of more or less a billion euros' worth of art, properties, and liquid assets was so meticulously preset to drain into two bankbooks that merely scrawling my initials in several pages' margins plugged the extra spigot.

In fact, our business meeting, with its high-speed shuf-fling of stapled pages, autographs, and touching anecdotes about the weirdo we would miss for somewhat corresponding reasons, might have been a courtesy, the lawyer told me, had not one faux pas caught his canvassing eye.

It seemed there was a gap amid my father's properties, spe-cifically a chateau framed by considerable acreage in the hills of Pas de Calais, a northernmost coastal area of France known exclusively to me for its hulking port and metro-like under-pinning of abandoned mines.

Unlike my father's other keepsakes, this effect lacked re-cords pertaining to its upkeep, taxes, or estimated value, and was not officially among my father's holdings, referenced only once and quickly in a handwritten note in one of the will's supplementary pages.

First thinking it a pure example of my father's riddles, the lawyer had halfheartedly typed a few search terms into Google and uncovered a solitary record of said property's existence—an item in the archives of the threadbare website of a razor-thin newspaper that served the nearest town.

Dated four or so years prior, the article sought to abridge a thickened curiosity among the town's two dozen residents regarding a peculiar-looking building that was then under construction on its westernmost fringe.

Quoting some hireling at the construction site, this article revealed the odd contraption's owner as a Parisian who bore my father's name. Notwithstanding the in-progress building's likeness to a theme park's far-off satellite, it was instead a children's playhouse, rooted there rather than in the owner's yard due to its enormity.

Upon completion, the playhouse would huff and puff an illustration in some comic book or other into three usable dimensions and become a walk-in birthday gift for the owner's younger son. Presumably, this boy would horse around within it on the weekends and over school vacations. Otherwise, it would gather dust and invite local teens' graffiti.

Most outlandishly, the owner had bypassed the normal practice of employing an architect to coax the inky streaks and dashes into solid matter. Instead, a cosmetic surgeon had been asked to make that difficult transition. The aim of this unorthodox approach, or so the worker said he'd heard, was that the playhouse would be less the drawing's souvenir or Disneyed offshoot than a twin of the unwrinkled thoughts behind it.

Wedged into one corner of the article was a low-resolution scan of the comic's panel that had formed the building's inspiration. My first impression, as I recall, was that the busy-looking, riotously structured prototype might have flourished in the wishy-washy first dimension, but it would surely topple at the onset of the first real breeze.

The only visible phone number on the website was in an ad noting a local florist, and so the lawyer dialed, reaching a loquacious woman who explained that, due to a recent fire, the flower shop was doubling as a pleasant-smelling city hall, and she was both a clerk and the town's elected mayor.

Yes, she knew of the unearthly building he described. Although once the superstar of local gossip, she said, its mysteries had grown unfashionable, due mostly to the dwelling's pitiable location off a barely traveled road that was, in truth, merely a driveway for the scattered homes along its edges.

However, not two weeks before the lawyer's call, the nutty edifice had made a kind of comeback when a stranger and his two sons started shopping at the local lumberyard.

The stranger, whose name she thought she'd overheard as Christophe or maybe Kristof, told the lumberyard's cashier his boys and he were houseguests at a manor in the area that he might know, at least by reputation, due to its unconventional façade.

Since that very lumberyard's stock of sawed-up trees had fed the budding structure, the cashier had its preposterous beginnings and backstory at his fingertips, and he repeated what he knew, both to be neighborly and to sound the stranger out.

While the cashier's tale was technically correct, the stranger said, it was also out of date. The building's owner was deceased, and his beloved son had disappeared not long before he'd died, abducted, it was thought, by his nanny, who'd also vanished, and whom authorities believed had raped and killed the child for, well, whatever reason pedophiles do horrendous things.

In happier times, this boy had, for no doubt goofy purposes, drafted a will, and with such neat penmanship and official-sounding turns of phrase that this document was fully legal. In his will, the boy had specified that, should he die, his playhouse would be passed down to the genius who'd designed it, and that genius, as luck would have it, was the very man addressing the cashier.

At that point, the mayor announced she had a bird of paradise in need of potting, but she would get in contact with the lawyer should any further scuttlebutt develop.

By the time the lawyer folded his computer, I was staring at the desk it left behind.

In hindsight, I was sappy to have thought myself immunized against my father's verbal daring-do, and to have blithely guessed that, as the only student of his tricks, I'd been plucked out of the audience, then put in charge of polishing his instrument.

For years, I had defined the marbled swarm to anyone who asked me why my father spoke in plusses as an over-stylization whose effect was no more threatening than the average villain's phony Russian accent.

Imagine if he typed his half of every conversation, I would posit. His teeth would be the keyboard and his tongue a fingertip. His tone of voice would be the font—a strange idea, granted, and yet planes weighing tons are often airborne—and that font would be, say, Webdings or another logotype whose concept trumps its information.

At worst, I would suggest, were my father in a shifty mood or over-caffeinated, and if you were on his schedule, you might hear yourself repay a compliment on your attire and find you'd placed the winning bid on van Gogh's *Sunflowers*, in effect.

That, in so many words, was how I thought I'd been instructed to employ this mannered spiel to which you've grown accustomed.

Hence, while I knew my father was a pompous, schmoozy motherfucker, I also saw the marbled swarm as hype against which he, the product, was overmatched, like, say, when Mel Gibson played Hamlet, which you might recall earned more money at the box office than every previous production of the play combined dating back to the seventeenth century, even though his version greatly displeased critics.

I'd been oblivious, or, to give myself a credit at which you are invited to balk, innocent—a kind of Robin who wasn't wedded to uncley Batman but rather hypnotized into an unwitting shadow of the Dark Knight—a carrier of the family tradition no truer to my father's grand designs than Alfonse's imitations were to mine.

One afternoon, the gendarme charged with rescuing Alfonse or producing his dead body from thin air confided that, while the case itself remained an open book, or a chapbook at the very least, his gut would like to say the boy was 86 percent deceased at last count.

No sooner had I locked my door, leaned heavily against it, and phoned François to share this reason to relax than my father texted me an invitation to share a dinner in his loft, ostensibly to reengage with the routine of family meals that my brother's predicament had discontinued.

As I was curious to know if, when sequestered with this most unavailable of parents, I might detect the hots I had assumed, or fantasized, if you prefer the God's-eye view, he nursed for me, I abided by his offer, likely with a smiley face emoticon, knowing how he hated such abbreviations.

For much of this high-powered meal, which replaced his coffee table's stack of Christie's catalogs with tins of Chinese take-out, my father's head, which I'll remind you looked a little like Gérard Jugnot's, starred the long face he had generally fastened to the world since my brother's truancy had left it hassled.

My face, by contrast, flirted, or, to add some color, nibbled at the turnip cakes astride my crisscrossed chopsticks with the seeping breaths and narrowed, witchy eyes of a young Brigitte Bardot dabbing suntan oil onto her cleavage.

While these efforts earned my crotch some cross checks and a throat clearance or two, our repartee itself maintained a roar of chews and gulps until my father deigned to ask about my day in the most bored voice you can imagine.

"Have you not observed, heard, and recorded for posterity enough of me already," I asked. "Perhaps my opinion of the Balenciaga shirt I bought this morning or a playlist of the new Muzak at Colette would sate the completist in you?"

As much as I would love to overrule some chums who've called my voice a kind of fancy drainage ditch through which my brilliant father's voice forever sloshes and evaporates, to ask myself to replicate his words verbatim would be like asking you to travel to Miami on the broken champagne bottle that baptized the ship that could have sailed you there in style.

Still, feel free to test what you've imagined the first printing of the marbled swarm entailed by clotting and annexing the phraseology that fills my cheaper trade edition.

In so many words, my father said that, were I to share this shopping trip with him, there was a chance his latent curiosity about the rue St. Honoré scene might be tweaked, although less by what I chose to say than by my belief that he would even be half listening.

"You will forgive me if I fall back on a gesture any idiot

my age might employ against his elders," I said, "but, to quote and qualify Rimbaud, I might defy you to prove that I do not contain multitudes."

My father said the reason I was taught the marbled swarm would be no different had he handed me a signed blank check and said, Here, make me penniless.

In fact, it was specifically to grant my squandered chance a second stimulus that he'd lighted into an experiment, which he understood François had slipped to me in crib note form and that he guessed I would expect him to substantiate.

I've edited the one-way conversation that ensued into a draft mundane enough to reach you, and while my text is surely not the half of his, it offers everything I understood. So, if the pages just ahead seem full of secrets and you notice them, I can tell you that I haven't, and any mindfucks are his.

One day, he said, he was hammering a Wim Delvoye untitled tattooed pigskin he'd recently acquired onto a wall in our old mansion when the nail flew through what he had incorrectly guessed would be a stubborn stretch of bricks.

When he'd withdrawn the nail, the tiny hole had emitted a veritable whistling wind, causing him sufficient wonder that he took to smashing it into a craggy maw through which he eventually inserted most of his head.

He surfaced not plugged into the wall itself but comfortably surrounded by what looked to be a secret room. After gutting the partition, he was able to climb inside this chamber with a flashlight, whose veering beam exposed a door, crudely hacked and with an archway so low-set it seemed to date from when Napoleon was not the dwarf we think today.

Naturally, my father ducked and entered, and, to save us time, discovered that the room was one of dozens that composed a crooked, hypodermal secondary house that interlaced the mansion's lodgings the way a tree's branches will twist and turn beneath their foliage.

A phone call to the former owner elicited a round of drinks, which lubricated a confession that, yes, he'd withheld the secret tunnels out of fear that, were the building's history to be included in the price, it would then be stained with disrepute, and he could never have retrieved his original investment.

He explained that in the 1930s, a man named Arval Benicoeur had resided in the mansion. Benicoeur was a notorious figure at that time due to claiming he had found the Marquis de Sade's infamously lost novel, *L'Egarement de l'infortune*. Sade had only undertaken *L'Egarement* to re-create *Les 120 journées de Sodome*, now his most commended work, which he'd written while confined in the Bastille and believed until his death had vanished in the prison's hasty if much celebrated storming.

Upon Sade's death, his moronic kin had burned the only copy of *L'Egarement*, causing every ersatz bookworm since to hope they'd been misquoted. It was this fabled manuscript that Benicoeur "discovered" in the very hidden passages my father had unearthed.

Shortly after making his outrageous boast, Benicoeur had disappeared, and a subsequent investigation of his abandoned house found no sign of the manuscript, much less the secret area from which he supposedly had dredged it.

Perhaps a dozen years later, a family by the name of Roux, who owned the mansion at the time, had a domestic spat. Things were thrown about, and something bashed a bedroom wall, and, thus, the house within the house had been accounted for.

Deep within it, a desiccated corpse bearing Benicoeur's distinctive nose was hanging by a noose. Parked against the walls around him, partially disassembled and locked in strange, tricycle-like positions, were fifteen skeletons, sized like children, each one showing evidence of tortures that appeared to match scenarios from Sade's extremist fiction.

Overflowing from a trash can near Benicoeur's shriveled feet were the wadded pages of a novel, written in an archaic form of French and scratched out with a feather pen that Sade could easily have used to chart his timeless horrors.

Ironically, this forged manuscript, the obsolescent pen, and any evidence of Benicoeur's crimes were victims of the fire that vaporized the archives of the Hotel de Ville in 1957, which was why his infamy was just a tidbit stuck on certain blogs and Facebook groups maintained by self-styled Sadeians.

Although this story had unnerved him, my father lacked the incredulity to seal the cursed tunnels. He'd kept them secret from his children not because he feared they'd give us nightmares, but because we might, if playing on the steep floors, break our little necks, and he'd only kept his wife out of the loop because the tunnels thrilled some women whom he fucked behind her back.

Once puberty had spiced me up and Alfonse could walk without gripping someone's pants leg—in other words, once we'd devised something akin to private lives—my father said he found himself shortening his time in our domain into a cameo, preferring to observe us more obliquely through the tunnels' wealth of peepholes.

One afternoon when we looked boring, and when my father had neglected to bring a book, he killed time by recollecting snatches of his childhood, notably his attendance at a performance, perhaps the very last, by a famous, then elderly French magician, to which my grandparents had brought him for his birthday.

The magic show featured numbingly familiar tricks to do with card decks, top hats, scarves, a scantily attired assistant sawed in two, and so forth, which the magician enacted with a certain itemized grace for which he'd been revered.

At some point, he'd made a showgirl vanish for several minutes. While her reemergence rolled my father's younger eyes, he said he'd felt disturbingly unworried while her disappearance was an issue.

Instead, he'd wondered what she would be thinking, poised backstage, he guessed, surely peeking through some curtain slit, waiting for her cue, watching strangers' eyes shred the stage in search of her, knowing that, in her nonexistence, she was briefly more important than the billion times more popular magician.

While my father thought the fad among psychologists of tracing clients' biases to childhood traumas was too Sherlock Holmes, he agreed that, while in the throes of this memory, he'd tagged that magic trick as the most likely animator of his wish to speak not in collegiate sentences, per se, but through fissures in a sonic curtain sewn from sentences' components.

For perhaps a year, the tedium with which Alfonse and I turned pages or made peculiar faces at cartoons managed to addict him, an entrancement he surmised had been related to his fondness for snail-paced French cinema of the early '70s.

But when our mother died so flashily while he was taxiing to CDG, the lack of impact from that ill-timed trip, and his newfound fear of missing anything again, had worked its offshoots into everything I saw around me, and that included who I thought I'd looked at in a mirror.

"If I might meddle in your indiscretions," I said carefully, "my current thought is that your purging lacks a certain moxie, perhaps owing to a qualm regarding sex talk and its hazards vis-à-vis the marbled swarm—a mismatch that, in my experience at least, causes me to no more speak my mind to listeners than one gives one's car to a mechanic."

To the contrary, my father said, he was guiding me behind his scenes in hopes of rescuing my theories from François's typically ribald interpretation.

He asked me to imagine he was the Paris Opera House. The time would be a century ago, and his voice the sound of Hector Berlioz conducting *Symphonie fantastique* once it had wafted through the lobby then fragmented in the ears of two bystanders lacking tickets, one a dedicated fan, who would represent myself, the other a spiteful peer of Berlioz, who would represent François.

As would be the case with any man whose closest friends were inevitably fathers of an adolescent son who wasn't wildly overweight, François's attentiveness whenever Alfonse was a noun could not be termed an act of listening but of meddling with his ears.

François was, to generalize, a kind of sex-crazed doppelganger of those crackpots in America who can't watch plates leave a waiter's hands without proclaiming that, if not for a government cover-up, they would have been UFOs.

"You'll pardon me," I said, "if I turn to a linguistic device I believe we both find favorable and less pose a question than construct its inner compound.

"If what you say is so, why would you cast the role of nanny as though Alfonse's need for laundered clothing was less realistic than a porn star's need for pizza delivery boys. Then there's the matter of your microscopic interest in my . . . let's say bedtimes, such that, when sharing your transcriptions with François, you quoted lines I surely wheezed more than enunciated and which must have barely swirled above my parted lips."

In this regard, my father said, I would need to choose between the flattery-cum-dispatch of François, who, he reminded me, was a chef prized for twisting honest, homely plants into forty-euro entrées, and his own confession, which was admittedly self-serving and, for that reason, as truthful as a poem is to its glazed-over scribe.

Still, as I seemed so inordinately smitten with the dirty lyrics in François's distorted cover version, he said he would expose one further fraction.

Yes, he'd fattened up our lofts with undisclosed locations and honeycombed the walls with lenses, but his experiments, and their sexual thematic in particular, were not the same fact-finding missions he'd undertaken in the mansion's less sophisticated setup, but . . . attempted murders, and when he'd zoomed into our crotches he might as well have lengthened the exposure until we whitened into nothingness.

"No doubt I'll bore us both by even daring to respond," I said. "Nonetheless, I must remind you these experiments, as articulating as they may have seemed to you, have occasioned certain dicey if not annulling end results, and I suggest this table's empty chair is one inescapable example."

At that, my father implemented several lurking, downcast facial muscles. He looked apologetic, even wounded, but I suppose in retrospect that anguish was as facetious as a monster mask's insanity.

First, as per the incest business, he said, had Alfonse's lifelong crush on me been any more embarrassing, and were I not so self-mesmerized that I treated his coquetry as opportunities to pick my own lock, the youngster would have burst into a circus clown with the onset of his pubic hair.

So, as dearly as he would love to give his master plan the credit, my father said our hanky-panky was a thing for which the term "God's work" had been devised, and his petty side effects had simply channeled me to move my ass, if I wanted to think about it that way.

As for Alfonse's death, that uncustomary outcome was the matter of a single word he hadn't vetted, a tiny gaff that had occasioned Azmir's failure to receive a minor signal he'd imbedded, armed, and holstered properly within its supervising sentence.

When he'd conceived the industriously garbled syntax he would call the marbled swarm, he knew it came with birthmarks that could leave its marvels cultish. Like most things French, whether candied chestnuts or every songbird save Piaf and Gainsbourg, its empire was restricted to the country's borders, former colonies, and some expatriates.

What he'd taken far too lightly was how the marbled swarm would fray whenever listeners weren't born and bred Parisians, eroding as their dialects had thickened. Since, in the majority of cases, the task assigned his voice was close to picking people's pockets with his mouth, he'd thought the missing subtleties were their loss, akin to listening to MP3s.

In the case of Azmir, although the tilted, dirtied French he'd grown up speaking in Algiers might strike the inattentive as no more weathered than the sludge that passed for conversation in Marseilles, it was, in point of fact, as far from French as Quebecois. Thus, a "don't" was born askew in Azmir's hearing, and, naturally, there was a domino effect once this mistaken "do" reached François's havoc-playing ears.

Still, in narrowing the murder suspects to a kingpin, he said my own faux pas were not acquitted, whereupon he compared my marbled swarm to bootleg records, as he called them—vinyl albums of substandard, say, Bob Dylan tunes whose crappy pressings had apparently bewitched the musicologist contingent of his dope-smoking generation.

One of these bootlegs, a crackly pileup of slapdash song stumps and snips of haywire instrumentals, had, in its inability to be judged fish or fowl, buttressed the legend of a never finished album known as *Smile*, whose humongous goal to make a recent Beatles LP sound archaic had turned its song-writer and producer into a drugged-out basket case before the project reached completion.

As in that rusty case, my father said the charms of my dis-organized recording of his sonic masterpiece were fair enough, but two miscues called for airing and unmasking in particular.

To originate the marbled swarm, he'd traveled conti-nents, retained selective habits from denominated countries' languages, then played with his infected voice for years. He'd blended half the world's linguistic greatest hits into the sinews of his French, adding octaves, subtracting clauses, until he could enunciate a fluent composition.

I, on the other hand, had slept a single night on one prefa-tory lesson that I'd likely been too stoned to intercept before hastily assembling my mangled swill.

I was very fortunate, he said, that Pierre Clémenti's genes had swamped my pleasant-looking mother's. For, while he'd long tagged Pierre's LSD trips as my maladjustment's guilty party, at least the actor's freakish sperm had stored the blue-print of his visage, because it was famously hard to judge someone while they were causing you to do a double-take.

He then assailed my so-called swill's techniques, damning in particular its misalignment of the marbled swarm's two paramount ingredients—namely, the French and English tongues.

Whether grouchily or because I'd watched too much imported television, my counterfeit had sidelined French as though its frills were parsley when, in the purer marbled swarm, our native language wasn't just a diamond mine of words that sought nationalists' protection, but a luscious broth wherein more splintered languages could be blurred and made subservient.

Here he quoted my late mother and supposed friends of mine, whom he conveniently left nameless since I have no actual friends, that while I talked like a pretentious frequent flyer from the States who had a good if fem French accent, at least I'd given his invention legs, even were they more like crutches.

As for my second noncompliance, I had derailed the marbled swarm with bathos, thereby baring its internal mechanisms to the mawkishness that made Americans such babies and had left, oh, Woody Allen, for example, a filmmaker who might have toppled Jacques Tati were his casts not such an unremitting string of whiny laughingstocks.

Had I learned the marbled swarm and not just cherry-picked its crust for wordplay and non sequiturs, the slushiness

I'd felt when killing Alfonse would have dried into an ennui masterminded and then thoroughly safeguarded by the French tongue's reflexive self-esteem.

Instead, by thinking Alfonse's silly feud with physics entailed his last request, my father said, I'd not just ruined a plan that had been intricate and in the works for years, I'd denied even his taste buds the symbolic father-son reunion he might have grudgingly accepted as a booby prize under those trying circumstances.

I should take a little stroll into François's walk-in freezer, he suggested, as he had done that very morning, and try to gaze with any interest whatsoever at the frosted throng of vaguely boy-like data crumpled in a corner.

Given this redressing, I'll declare myself tactical enough to have returned even imaginary fire. "Intricate plan," I managed to croak, "a phrase I'm now supposed to sweep from its surrounding wordage like your janitor and then dissect atrociously."

My father tightened his chopsticks into the classic v and plucked a dim sum from the only envelope-like carton that could still be called a smokestack.

If I wished my life to compensate me, he said, I was advised that, when something inexplicable occurred, or if too many things seemed unbelievable at once, were I to sense in one of them the affect of my father's handiwork, or, were the mystery a human, to suspect my father's mind had magically usurped that person's skull, then pursuing it or he or she would form the wisest and most Byzantine decision.

As I had chosen all my life to mince where he'd sashayed, my mind pawing thoughts his cognizance had long since vacuum sealed and gilded, I was no more fit to supervise my life without his steerage than were I some stray dog coaxed out of a crate in the middle of the wilderness.

He offered me a nightcap in the form of a prefabricated clue, whereupon, deleting first his voice and then the look of pity from his eyes, he mouthed a word I totally misread for months as "Châtelet," thinking, quite understandably, that the most involuted, tangly, confusing metro stop in Paris would do the work of six or seven hints combined.

In the few remaining weeks before his death, I pushed stepladders to my loft's foreboding walls then seesawed atop them, magnifying glass in hand, one ear cemented to the bottom of a drinking glass.

I spoke tightly when I was home, and I had sex I wouldn't pay myself to have again, ears perpetually straining toward those poisoned walls, hoping, I suppose, my father's lustful mewls might pierce their insulation.

Then my father was discovered sleeping just this side of death in his apartment, where one random wall was noticed to be strangely jutting open. No sooner had his gurney turned an ambulance into an earthbound jet than I hunted down a flashlight and raced through the impromptu door.

The so-called secret headquarters that François had described was just a storage room crammed with sculptures wrapped in belts of plastic sheeting, and their ghostly first impression was by far the oddest thing about the place.

While a staircase did descend from one corner of the room, it was a creaky metal fire escape that had traversed the building's western side for centuries until Philippe Starck shoved it underneath one of his signature barren façades.

It was then I understood the marbled swarm was not the act of terrorism I'd imagined but instead a method or procedure to keep the world intact, altered not one physical iota, while talking oneself into believing words alone could customize it.

To illustrate this convoluted point, let's say we reconvene back at the meeting with my father's lawyer. He and I conducted business in the largest of my loft's six rooms, although they're more like subdivisions of one giant room than isolating sections. His laptop, a PowerBook G4, as I recall, rested on a glass-top desk, and we watched the slideshow on its desktop from the comfort of a gray French Empire couch.

From there, one has an unobstructed view of Pierre Huyghe's *This Is Not a Time for Dreaming*, a video in which string puppets stage the life of Le Corbusier, and partially obstructed views of Philippe Parreno's *Fraught Times*, a high-rise decorated Christmas tree cast in aluminum, as well as Jean-Marc Bustamante's *Larva 1*, which looks exactly like it sounds.

Now, pretend I could transport you there as my invited guest. Upon materializing, you would search the premises for me, of course, and I might introduce myself since you could never spot me otherwise, whereupon, and this I promise, you would gawk and squint and rubberneck, then mutter to yourself that I look nothing, literally nothing like you'd pictured.

You might nose around the room and say, "It's more a garret than a loft, and where's this lawyer and his laptop or the art you keep alluding to," and, turning to a window, if you could even find one without settling for a pinhole, declare the view outside most definitely not Parisian.

Eventually, your eyes would rest on undistinguished me, sitting primly in my gray-scale world, and you might ask, "How could you have imagined there were secret passages behind these yellowed, close-knit walls, or have believed yourself unique enough to spy upon?"

And I would say to you, "But you are in the secret passage now," and, even as you read those words, you think I'm trying to revise the things I've said into a lie or obfuscation, but I guarantee that, were we together, you would understand my point exactly, which I realize is no help whatsoever.

Does a magician's trick lie about the top hat in which a card appears to vanish? Is a cartoon lying about the computers on which it was laboriously hatched? Does your favorite song lie to you about the badly dressed musicians who sang and strummed and tinkered it into a tune while separated from each other's work by days or months and soundproofed booths?

In both the marbled swarm founded by my father and the marbled junk I've siphoned off, there is no lie or contradicting truth you need to fear. Neither are there plural truths or lies you need to worry you'll discover, much less keep apart or in a special order.

If I've made the headway I intend, you have endured my story's stiffened pages knowing I would puzzle out the mysteries they keep demarking, but you are starting to suspect that, all this time in which you lent my characters and anecdotes the benefit of liveliness, you've just been reading what you want to read.

Since I've refreshed the meeting with my father's lawyer, let me catch you up beginning there. I walked him out, pushed "Down," and, as the elevator's portal sealed, offered to search Alfonse's bedroom for a will that might have left some playhouse in or near Calais to some cosmetic-surgeon-slash-moonlighting-architect.

Once the elevator emptied him, I took a turn in the

contraption, then unlocked Alfonse's loft, using what had been his key because he'd iced it with a rubber silhouette of Pikachu, which made the object easy to distinguish from the euro coins that always bottled up my pockets.

Technically, the loft was Didier's, or, since its official owner at that moment was a bank, I guess it would be prudent and more accurate to say it was his hideout, given that our building's entrance code and several bolt locks guarded him against François, whom I was worried at the time had secret plans to murder him, then hide the body on our forks, long story short.

Still, the loft was even less a fort in practice than a spacious red light district wherein Didier formed the only showpiece, a change of scene that will require an explanation, I suppose, so, unfortunately, the doorknob can't be turned until I've backed this story up into an unfamiliar circumstance again.

Should you find that prospect tiring in advance, you might counteract my backwash with a daydream wherein I— and you can use the young Pierre Clémenti circa *Belle du Jour* as your referral—am frozen at a steel, flat-panel door, intoning not the afterthought to follow but a lengthy password of the fancy sort that musketeers in fairy tales must chant to shift a cliff into some hush-hush kingdom's craggy entrance.

When my father died, Crédit Mutuel's policy of freezing clients' assets for the length of their estates' protracted settlements cut off my allowance. François, who could easily have fronted me the weekly three thousand euro on which I'd grown dependent, and before whom I sat myself one humbled afternoon, regarded my politely folded, nearly praying hands with his usual mischievousness.

Claiming he was skint after taking up the slack of Azmir's salary, he said it might both serve my stated purpose and revive a nasty if nostalgic habit were we to, oh, pretend I was a pimp of all amusing things and Didier my whore who, through some miracle or other, brought to mind his younger son but had no resonance, thanks to the chilling side effect of capital.

He then produced the names of friends and restaurant clientele whom he was certain would pay lavishly to sleep with any Northern European twelve-year-old, much less some coddled little bitch like Didier, who could have easily homogenized into the freshman class of Hogwarts, even if the character he most resembled was Ron Weasley.

Didier was brought before us, made to strip and turn in halting circles as he discarded garments, play air guitar, do calisthenics, and so forth, while François and I made note of what he was unknowingly conveying when our crotches most reminded us of pets begging for scraps at a dinner table.

Knowing what I've let you gather, need I even rehash my opinion that his greatest shot at getting laid, by me at least, was with the help of Emo, both for the pinpointed reason that

I dug the type and a more practical conjecture—i.e., given the speed with which porn stars of every build and age were Emo-fying at the time, it seemed that gay guys no more cared which Emo did the job than we might care which eggs were in our omelets.

The next morning, Didier was cloistered in a high chair at the Toni & Guy flagship salon on rue St. Honoré while François and I browbeat a stylist until he'd trimmed, blackened, and gelled the boy's mousey, unkempt mop into a kind of windswept burqa, or as close as hair's anemia could take and wouldn't force the boy to poke at his surroundings with a white cane.

After a lenient tip, we picked the stylist's brains for his opinion on this newborn Emo's chances as a school-yard Lorelei. "Few," he said unhesitatingly, citing Didier's hairline lips and feral case of "glass eye syndrome" as the biggest culprits, although he added that a decent pair of tinted contact lens might tease some IQ points into his deadpan marbles.

His little inconveniences could be refined, the stylist said, but, barring headlines from the world of medicine, his looks would gall until such time as head transplants were feasible. Still, if we cared to dig a few last ditches, he knew a surgeon who could crib the chin and knock a centimeter off the forehead, and we might consider starving him in case his face was hiding cheekbones.

Originally, we'd planned to cab from the salon to a nearby April 77—i.e., a storefront in a trendy chain of Emo clothing stores whose founder, if you're interested, had gambled that the newly christened Emos might eventually join the Punks in fashion's annals, and, if so, that they would need a more coherent statement than the Cure T-shirts and holey jeans worn by the movement's pioneers.

But, while Didier's repackaged head drew less attention from what was, in truth, a perfectly attractive torso, it also made his greatest selling point look . . . well, fat is pushing it, but, in any case, we chose to take a chance and edit his physique into something artier and less commercial.

His daily food intake was clenched into a single bite, causing the famished boy to topple furniture and wreck expensive artworks in search of baguette flakes, which is why the devolution of a sculpture by the artist Carsten Höller into a figurative cage dates from this period.

While Didier withered, François handcuffed our gestating Cinderella once a week and taxied to some clinic in the seventeenth arrondissement, where a patron of L'Astrance who earned his keep by smothering old actors' skulls with their own saggy faces would crop and trim the boy in trade for discounts at our incubating whorehouse.

I think it was a Monday when Didier grew too enfeebled to fight his sharp-edged figure, listless speech, and dragging gait, and felt sufficiently depressed to think black eyeliner was a brand of fairy dust and that he couldn't look sickly and thin enough.

At the nearby corner of rues Normandie and Saintonge, April 77 had just opened its gazillionth store, and we asked its clerk to help us crossfade Didier into an Emo who could name-check Tokio Hotel without suspicion, but would feel no more beholden to his outfit than a girl who tries on edible underwear to celebrate her boyfriend's birthday.

If my fetish for rerouting even sentences that plummet at their points into Chinese puzzles makes my dawdling on this Emo renovation seem numbingly fiducial, let me add that while the reasons Didier and I became an item in the next few days are overly complex, I can't discount the way he looked in drainpipe jeans, which is strange.

Now, with that cinch of narrative in place, I'll return us to the afternoon weeks hence when, if you'll remember, I suggested that the spitting image of the young Pierre Clémenti might bedeck the doorknob of Alfonse's former loft if you so wished.

If by chance this chronicle has been adapted for the radio by France Culture, and you are listening instead of reading, you will likely hear a noise that, although created by a wooden shingle with a loose, protruding nail, screams "creaking door." But had the door in question creaked, I might have been five hundred euro in the red, since Didier's most recent client, a government attache of the Czech Republic embassy, as I recall, had grossly overrun his hour-long appointment.

I traced the duo through a spray of coins and fallen cutlery, past a coffee table that had been overturned and looked as gluey as a newborn painting, to a sculpture—Haruki Murakami's *My Lonesome Cowboy*, if you know it or that matters—which was jiggling suspiciously and venting moans not three steps from where I gently closed the door behind me.

As I mentioned, Didier spent his late nights, work breaks, and all unsupervised time moseying about inside a grid-like sculpture that had had some cogitative rationale for only looking like a cage before I literalized the reference with a prisoner and padlock.

I bring this up again not to gloss my villainous or conscientious sides, but to plumb the mystery of why, despite the loft's reanimation as a copious illegal sex club, Alfonse's bedroom was still the chipper nursery he had left behind on what must constitute the world's worst ever date and birthday gift combined.

His computer screen was still a breezy, ceaseless mosh pit swirled with laughing flowers. The surface of the eco-friendly bamboo desk on which it whirred and drawers yielded nothing more official than his usernames and passwords. I power-squeezed each pair of socks, balled or not, wrung the gist out of his underwear, pajamas, pants, and every T-shirt wavering in his closet.

I advanced upon the bookshelves, where Alfonse had wedged his zillion manga, and which would not have been a piece of cake to pry apart in any case, even had each booklet's gaudy, unmarked spine not crashed its borders and conjoined to form a brazen mural that caused my allergy to stimuli to flare and left my usually acerbic eyes the equivalent of candles.

I was cringing at those rows and rows without the where-withal to yank apart and ruffle through the concourse book by book, when I noticed something that was neither pink nor especially stimulating jutting from one manga's upper crust.

I slid the manga from its tight spot and opened to the bookmarked page, no doubt whistling between my teeth or something of that flummoxed nature when the denoted illustration showed the same synopsis of a playhouse that had originally sent me on this treasure hunt, minus some graininess.

Then there was the matter of the bookmark. It was, in lay-men's terms, a postcard sent to Alfonse four years earlier and postmarked in Calais—if, that is, I read its smeary marks and peeling stamp correctly.

On the blanker of the card's two sides, there was a scribbled phrase whose ornate diction could be traced back to my father's. While my adaptation of its message is a fling, the words were something very close to "Use this card to find the entrance."

In the space below, my brother had inscribed his father's name, my mother's, mine, and "Alfonse." Each was followed by a dash and then a different name that seemed to correspond, at least to his imagination, and none of which I recognized that afternoon, but you would.

The bookmarked manga, which I paged through mindfully for, all told, an hour, had lifted everything but its perverseness from the oft-retold and readapted children's bedtime story known, at least in France, as "The Three Bears."

For instance, Goldilocks was neither girl nor boy but rather a little sissy with ellipsoid eyes whose tartan culottes hid a whopping penis. The tempting dinner bowls held soba noodles, and the cozy-looking beds were skimpy mats. The family of bears didn't welcome their intruder with a party then pay for her train fare back to Paris, like in the version I remember.

Instead, being bears not in the corny, aw-shucks sense to which we're accustomed, but biologically, they swatted Goldilocks awake then spent a dozen pages screwing him or her, which, with the strange propriety that puts the Japanese among the earth's most civilized degenerates, required every sort of smudge or nearby flowerpot to blot their intersecting crotches.

Once Goldilocks was clawed and squashed by accident into reliquiae too vile to give an animal a boner, the bears, whose thinking had been compromised or tamed to some degree by the human clothes in which their illustrator squared them, chose not to chomp and shred him/her into a ragged snack.

After juggling their spoils into the kitchen, the baby bear boiled sticky rice, the mama bear docked sheets of seaweed into sushi wrappers, and the papa bear nicked clods of raw material from the body's open wounds with his impressive nails.

Soon, California rolls were crowded on a varnished wooden plank, whereupon they ate until their snoring, newly pregnant-looking bodies hit the kitchen floor, human bones still drooping from their paws like they were narcoleptic drummers.

My fingertips were hyper-tapping on the manga's cover when I noticed Didier was standing in the doorway of my brother's room, one hand holding out a slew of fifty-euro bills, the other playing with his petty but impregnable erection.

Back when I felt vaguely certain I was gay, I dipped into the so-called dungeon of Le Depot one stoned night and quickly realized men would gather there not in order to give blow jobs in the dark, per se, but to have sex with a darkness wherein they formed no more than sets of circumstances.

I believe those lurking men refer back to these underground collisions as their "things." Things, I would guess, as opposed to memories.

Anyway, point is, I had been doing "things" with Didier in recent weeks.

Let me remind you that, while I've filtered apparitions of my colleagues' speaking voices, minus one or two, as I consider them less friends of mine or yours than my ingredients, to muzzle Didier would be like hooking a police badge on the T-shirt of a kid who likes to hang around police stations.

"That asshole didn't even try to get me off," Didier said. "So much shit about my loins and their profound elixir, and then it was just, 'Swallow what you made, you stupid whore.'"

"Let me pose a question," I said, "and precede it with a caveat, which is to say your answer will influence my decision to assist you with your issues or continue with my day."

"François says you're just a boring, pretentious piece of shit," Didier said, "but maybe because I'm stupid, I think it's more like listening to classical music."

"You'll recall Alfonse," I continued, "the Flatso you betrayed, misled, murdered circumstantially, and whose human infrastructure used to live here. So, were you, Azmir, and I to embark upon a road trip to Calais, of all lackluster places, to find a man who knew Alfonse by reputation, do you think you could impersonate my brother in his presence and repeat a fib that you were kidnapped, raped, and blah blah blah, which I would first devise then have you memorize?"

I was midway through this question when the portion of

my sight as yet unclouded by the culinary fantasies I find it useful to construct before attempting sex noted a sort of glitch or break in Didier's familiar grumpiness.

"Holy shit," he said, or rather yelled, or even shouted joyfully, I'll dare to say. He started fingering his face's redesign, which, in just the last few days, had finally trimmed and decked his cussedness into a stubborn curve or two. "So, that's what all this bullshit is about."

Among the minor features of Alfonse's bedroom was a mirror, where he would stand and stare back at his wistful, flattened looks for hours, a painful memory I'd buried in my posttraumatic stress until Didier turned left and saw almost the very same reflection.

"It's like I fell off a skateboard," he said, "and my face got mangled, and when they sewed it back together, they fucked up and used a picture of your brother as the map instead of me."

Has my tendency to call an orange a tangerine prepared you to believe that, with a dutiful cosmetic surgeon and François's agnate taste in boys as my assistants, I'd been engraving Alfonse in Didier sans any knowledge of my motives whatsoever? I ask because it happens to be true.

What could have been more natural—or more "me" at least—than to have viewed the carnage in François's garage as a problem with my eyesight, then simply changed perspectives like my father might have traded peepholes until I found an angle on Alfonse that flattered him again.

I'm sure I mentioned how, if Alfonse had found Emo's depressions as engaging as Japan's idolatry of printed people, he might be here today and so adored by suitors who appreciate asocial conduct when it's properly attired that I would seem as phony and impossible to love as I suppose I really am.

I'll remind you one last time about my stroll with Serge across the chateau's woodsy yard, wherein I speed-judged his admissibility as food and found him hollow enough.

Now I'll suggest that, were you to rejuvenate that scene's environs as window dressing then imagine I was ranking Serge's fitness as my brother's clotheshorse, I could easily have told you I was here with Didier that day learning to accept Alfonse's likeness, and, as you may have even gathered by this point, I was.

I slept horribly, and yet my iPhone's silent, rumbling alarm so piqued my minor interest in exploring day-lit rooms and views, it might have played my favorite TV program's theme song if the show in question weren't predictably *Twin Peaks* and were its overture less soporific.

While feeding grounds into my coffeemaker and setting it to stun, I sent François, Olivier, and Azmir texts whose predicating pings were half the battle, since the notes just nudged them to assemble in my loft more hurriedly than planned.

Still, by the time I'd had one of my all-or-nothing showers then taxed my caffeine buzz with a strangely complicated question of which McQ blue long-sleeve western shirt to wear, my lack of sleep had bogged my shoelaces and buttons into rusty cranks and broken knobs.

Once I joined my colleagues, all of whom were baggy-eyed and blazoned with the wet, smeared hair of recent swimmers—well, excluding Didier, who looked precisely as he did when I had locked him in his cage hours before, which is to say like Alfonse if my brother had been a hiking trail beloved by snails—I was less their peppy leader than a fellow dawdler lying prostrate over one of Philippe Starck's curvilinear, back-breaking chairs.

François thought a summons to his coke dealer seemed in order. It was a capital idea, or would have been were we not still convalescing from a forty-eight-hour-long "afternoon" of accidental binging when we'd found my father's secret coke stash in our spoonfuls of Corn Flakes three days before.

I'll retrieve this incident beginning at the point where, having polished off my bowl, I was spurred into an even more than usually exasperating nitwit who licked and ground my teeth while using them to air my every thought and scrabbling my ring of house keys like a rosary.

Having learned the night before that Alfonse's so-called will was just a postcard cryptogram, I phoned my father's lawyer, and, since my pell-mell vocal patterns clipped the news into an outburst, and given that his rates were hourly, he proposed I cede the fifty-five remaining minutes to the mayor whom he had quoted at our meeting, and I agreed on the condition that he phone me back with the address of the supposed playhouse so I could plug it into Google Earth.

I'd planned to kill the almost-hour fingering some phone apps whose offbeat missions and designy logos had put the make on my contracted pupils.

Still, as coke can't seem to help but use its hopheads to accomplish, I found a quiet study of these apps beyond me, and soon enough my antsy friends and I were in a huddle, having misconstrued our need to chatter as the impetus for lectures and confused one another for captivated listeners at whom we could not spew enough.

For my part, I chronicled Pierre Clémenti's oeuvre, complete with capsule plots of every title, which is a tribute either to the marbled swarm or to coke's divinatory powers, since my knowledge of his films was almost limited to YouTube clips, and, even in those cases, they were fan-made compilations of his shirtless scenes with power-ballad soundtracks.

When the lawyer took a costly ninety minutes–plus to ring me back, I didn't seem to care because another ten or twelve minutes blitzkrieged by before the cocaine let him say a word.

He'd reached the mayor, but, before an opportunity arose to wrest the street address, she literally thanked God for the reoccurrence of his stiff, familiar tones, and, in a voice warped by her anxiousness and thickset northern accent, told him a story he would re-create as best he could given that his habit was to translate people's ranting into clear-cut legalese.

She'd said a fourteen-year-old local boy had turned up missing. Around their comfy town, this boy was known if not beloved as the skittish, twitchy, slit-eyed urchin whose seeming lack of ancestry and favorite perch outside the district's sex shop had troubled every glimpse of him.

Townsfolk guessed he was the castoff of a widowed, alcoholic former miner who would rarely leave his shack out by the highway and whose standoffishness and gone-to-seed good looks seemed the likely birthplace of this fugitive yet unassuming child.

Earlier that year, the town's rapscallion, Quinton Dupont, aged fifteen, had befriended the uncordial boy. Quinton's mother was so pleased to think her naturally combatant son might have an altruistic streak that she allowed the boy to curl up nightly in the family tool shed.

But there had been a recent falling out between the boy and Quinton. To the township, it seemed one of those contretemps that halve the sturdiest of teenage chums, until, that is, Mrs. Dupont, who was known to everyone but local children as Aimee, began to worry aloud and quite incessantly.

She would insist to anyone who greeted her that, in the weeks since this disbandment, Quinton had fallen into something she believed from reading Paris newspapers was called depression. He ate minutely, could only seem to think and speak of his detached friend, while, at the same time, clamming up whenever what's-his-name was made the topic of a question.

As for the twitchy boy, he'd not been seen in town for weeks, causing locals to surmise that, having gained a fondness for companionship, he'd reconciled with his reclusive father. This blind guess had grown lazily official since, apart from Quinton, townsfolk felt his exit only made the streets seem cleaner and less emotionally taxing to navigate.

But on the very afternoon the mayor and advocate had spoken last, Aimee rushed into the flower shop, panting that, while window shopping at the lumberyard that morning, she'd seen the freakish family that, as gossip had it, were residing in "the bauble," as locals sometimes called the weird abandoned playhouse.

While the man and boys had proved to be the rumored eyesores, she said the younger of the sons had bothered her particularly. As she had pleasant memories of watching *Edward Scissorhands*, she used his countervailing innocence to reassure herself, then forced her gaze to parse the child's vampiric coif and outfit, and, the less they formed her view, the more he seemed to reproduce or even be the boy who'd left her son a basket case.

She'd lingered in the lumberyard's small gift shop, handling its wooden replicas of nearby points of interest, until the strange child fled his family long enough to scrutinize a tiny hand-carved skeleton, whereupon she swooped, so increasingly convinced her guesswork was correct with every clarifying footstep that she called to him the way she always had—i.e., "Hi, Quinton's friend."

With that, the boy looked up to see his ex-friend's mother, and, as his heavily mascaraed eyes were widening, he'd snapped the skeleton in half. The crack of bursting lathwork carried through the shop, drawing a mistrustful glance from his alleged father, at which point Aimee had retreated out the entrance.

She'd driven home, hoping to soothe Quinton with her discovery. Instead, startled by this news from his familiar fetal pose upon the bathroom floor, he'd requested a La Bière du démon from the fridge, which seemed to her a good sign, then downed the bottle in one wobbling gulp, which didn't.

One day, Quinton said, back when he and the peculiar boy were best of friends, a nosy mood beatified by several Red Bulls each had made them want to scale a tattered section of the brick-and-barbed-wire battlement that fenced the legendary playhouse.

No sooner had they thudded to their feet inside the compound than the dust raised by their landing breezed into the view of what would have been the hottest girl on earth, he said, were "she" not exercising at that moment dressed in skin-tight leotards.

This feminine, mirage-like boy introduced himself as Claude, the only offspring of the man whose property they'd just transgressed. Despite his disappointing penis, he balanced out as quite a decent guy by giving them permission to have a full-fledged look around.

As he attempted to describe the playhouse to his mother, Quentin's sentences had quilled like Chinese acrobats and rat-a-tatted like contestants in a high-stakes spelling bee and finally crashed his voice into the feedback necessary to enunciate such words as "mind-boggling" and "insane" with sufficient majesty.

Still, he said the weirdest thing was Claude's supposed father, whom he'd never seen in so much as shadow. Due to some medical condition Claude had somehow lengthily yet barely managed to explain, his father couldn't breathe the same oxygen as everybody else.

Thus, he'd supervised their visit from some unknown room and through at least one hidden camera. When he'd spoken to and with them, a voice had burbled from a speaker in the wall, as though they were an all-male Charlie's Angels or three versions of that guy in *Saw* who sawed his leg off to escape.

The boy and he had started hanging out there daily, and Quentin said he couldn't quite explain its staying power unless . . . the father's fun suggestion that the boys perform a play for his amusement had not eventually devolved into a thing that seemed less fun in retrospect.

Quentin guessed the play's interminable length might have engineered some kind of trance, as it was written to be acted out in real time, day after day, morning until evening, not to mention its enthralling story line, which had narrowed their attention like the stages of the Tour de France.

Among the play's tight cast of characters was a man of roughly middle age and no profession who, like Claude's elusive father, made no appearance on the stage itself, although this subterfuge was due not to a medical condition but to his secretive and morbid curiosity.

Then there was the man's dead wife, although her corpse, which spent its face time lying crumpled on a staircase, only seemed to be a facet of the play to show how he had forged two of his ejaculations into sons.

The most important characters were, first, the couple's younger son, a suicidal fourteen-year-old liar who swanned around the stage in Emo outfits, and, second, a cute but tiresome young adult from Paris who was in the play for reasons no one understood, not even him.

The play was set in a chateau whose history of on-site murders, ghosts, and other unexplained phenomena required a lengthy spoken foreword, which Claude's father had recited through the speakers for what would have felt like months were not the bloodthirsty details of this story custom-made for mordant teenagers.

To cite the most agentive of these details, the couple's older son had either killed himself, been murdered, died by tragic accident, or faked his death within the previous few months.

The anguished man and wife had put the crime scene on the market, and the young Parisian, struck by certain parallels between their son's obituary in *Le Monde* and the clueless death of his own brother years before, found himself inspired to visit the chateau and then acquire it.

While touring his purchase, he'd discovered there was more to the chateau—specifically its riddling with secret passageways—and to the family, whose screwiness seemed less a legacy of grief than the bluff of incommunicado people, than had been mentioned by the building's real estate agent.

However, even he became a suspect when, after sealing the transaction with a handshake, he kidnapped the son, an act that might have offered them relief, considering their offspring's pricey regimen of meds, were he not a resident of the Marais, which even people in the provinces had heard was overrun with homosexuals.

Claude's father's disembodied voice had played the patriarch, of course, as well as reading out the stage directions where required. Claude was cast in two small roles that proved quite meaty when combined, that of the older, dead or missing son in flashbacks, and the frozen but dramatically positioned mother's corpse.

The twitchy boy portrayed the younger son, since it was thought his scrawniness would bring an Emo artifice to life and that his meek, unkempt behavior might misread as suicidal in the costume's gloomy envelope.

Quentin was awarded the Parisian's role, and he admitted having relished his alter ego's evil, violent streak so wholly that he hadn't minded all the homework it required to nail the character's bombastic speech and la-di-da comportment, not that watching DVDs of Monty Python skits dubbed into French was work.

Quentin swore the play was such a corkscrewed mass of crisscrossed plots and episodic pickles that he hadn't even noticed when a gay subtext curtailed its breakneck pacing with some icky love scenes whose X-rated realizations might not have been so crucial to maintain the work's integrity in hindsight.

Still, the play was so ingenious that learning what new twist the Emo's death might trigger seemed more important than not murdering a friend, and it was only when the gory scene was under way that Quentin lost it, grabbed his woozy, battered costar by his hoodie's blood-soaked sleeve, and ran away, not even stopping when he felt the Emo costume slip or wriggle free.

The mayor was as astonished by this yarn as Quentin's mother, but the district's scandals were her duty. So, with a phone call, she dispatched the town's patrolmen to the property, and, after taping a "Closed" sign to the window of the bakery that doubled as their station, they'd bathed Main Street in gushes of revolving lights and yapping sirens so unheard of in those restful parts that many locals have suggested it become an annual event.

Excepting Quentin, no one in town had ever seen the finished playhouse, and the mayor declared that, had she thought to tape the gendarmes' whimpering account of its emergence from the trees, it might have made the famous coverage of the Hindenburg disaster sound fastidious.

Having recently been out to see the playhouse for herself, she claimed her words were far too pinched to do its dynamism justice. Still, one of her descriptions, which had turned a local drunk into a churchgoer, might be a starting place, she said, but it relied on Euro Disney to make its point, to which the lawyer assured her he'd been dragged there by his nieces.

First, she said he should remember, say, two dozen of the park's wildest attractions. Then, he should imagine they were stacked, one vulgar ride atop another, to create a sort of garish, thick-necked totem pole whose height would dwarf the Eiffel Tower's.

Next, he should imagine the gigantic hand of God was fading in above the column and then pressing down with all His mighty strength. Since God was the greatest of magicians, the stack would not be crushed into debris. Instead, the highest ride would wondrously merge into the one below, and that mutated ride would blend into the next, and so forth, until what occupied the ground was an unearthly, massive doodad.

Now, to reengage with the investigating cops, they'd parked their squad car, battled through the building's psychedelic headwinds, distinguished a front door of sorts, kicked it in, and drawn their flashlights.

Rather than the honeycombed infinity of rooms foreshadowed by the tangled outer shell, what faced their evanescent firing squad was just one very plain, enormous, empty space.

The walls, floor, and ceiling weren't the friendly, decorated borders of a home, but rather raw wood sheets that brought to mind some kind of epic packing crate in which another house had been delivered.

Still, having tracked their share of UFOs back to a moonlit water tower, the gendarmes searched the room in the name of an investigation, and they would have found nothing abnormal had the concept of normality applied and were the younger cop not prone to sweat when he was disconcerted.

Mistaking a grainy slat of wall for possible graffiti, the younger cop approached this seeming clue, and, while he stood admiring nature's unkempt artistry, he felt a highly welcome coolness whish and climb his hairy legs.

Crouching both to analyze the source and dry himself, he realized that a draft of air was infiltrating a small folio of floorboards, and yet his snooping flashlight found no markings of a trap door or repairs that might explain it.

After handcuffing the busted playhouse door, they'd driven out to see the alcoholic miner, but he'd stopped their squad car in the driveway with a rifle, shouting, "Son, what fucking son." He'd lost his manhood in a knife fight when he was seven, he explained, and if they'd wondered why he drank so much, he was drunk enough to drop his pants and educate them.

Their next stop was Aimee's home, where they'd interrogated Quentin, hoping that their firsthand knowledge of the playhouse would compel him to retract his lies, or, should he have gone insane, disillusion him. Instead, he'd quickly reemerged as the disrespectful hooligan who liked to bugger homeless cats with lighted fireworks for quote-unquote no reason.

They'd locked him in the nearest to a jail cell that their station-cum-bakery could fake, meaning the closet where they stored their vacuum cleaner, but, after studying the junk in there all afternoon, the playhouse in his stories sounded, if anything, even more Byzantine and pornographic.

In the mere few days since then, the mayor said, time seemed to have rewound a month. The peculiar father-son team had left town or escaped into the mines, and, if so, were surely dead by now or wandering in ever-slower circles.

The single aspect of the strange, chimeric incident not chalked up to Quentin's bullshit or the paranoid delusions that piggyback small towners' boredom was the nameless boy or, given no one knew him in the first place, his whereabouts.

That case would likely stay unsolved by any tricks within their means, the mayor said, barring a leak from Quentin's shrink. Still, a photo of the missing boy, if it was him, that had been lifted off the lumberyard's surveillance footage, was now posted on the town's official website, although it showed a face more heavily made-up than easily made out.

When I re-latched my iPhone's leather case, it could have been a castanet, since my companions, having found my drawn-out silence shocking, literally busted out in raucous dance steps, fueled by cocaine's tickles and their curiosity to know what could have muted me.

First, I ducked into my office, woke a desktop, launched Safari, and then fed it search terms like "Calais," "nearby," and "playhouse," until one link unpeeled a site that I reloaded several times before my browser aced the geriatric code that left it knotted up with animated gifs and clip art.

The power of bad photographs to sculpt old bedsheets into ghosts of World War casualties is known to every half-sane TV addict, and the missing boy's photo required a vicious squint to tell him from its surface noise, but, I swear, had Alfonse been corporeal or were Didier a twin, I could have been studying either one of them.

More important, I was certain that—and, if I've laced my story tightly, you've been cursing my slow-wittedness for pages—given the classified, surveying father and his sketchy, bit-part children, and . . . well, every aspect—even its provincial chateau setting—as "chateau" was just two letters shy of "Châtelet," which was my father's final clue to me, as you'll recall—if the play in Quentin's story wasn't an imaginative lie, its author was most certainly my father.

Granted, he'd never even canonized my mother in a sappy poem, or none that she had pinned onto the fridge, but, then again, all his fulsome talk of how he'd bagged a billion euro from a bunch of idiots had never held my interest, nor would I likely have picked up on any chitchat about the Comédie-Française or the Festival d'Avignon or things like that.

I've mentioned my discrediting performance as an acting student when an adolescent, and I'll hope you paused there long enough to guess I wouldn't reference that and make myself a laughingstock to you without first giving my little sacrifice a saving grace.

A day would come, and one minutely less historic than the afternoon I'm re-creating, when filling dinner plates with almost anyone I wished to kill, abbreviate, and season proved even less conducive to my talents than the acting jobs I might have nailed had they been custom-built with me in mind.

Human food is such a chore to edit, involving such a surfeit of accomplices, stranding so much eerily familiar, shoddy chaff that proves so humdrum to partition from the nest eggs and then fade away from the police.

It would begin to pain me that, if I remained a cannibal or viewed myself as one, I would never have the independence of an actor who can disappear into his body as behind a puff of smoke or the freedoms of an artist who need only find an isolated room to make his magic and then pay the rent and close the door.

One of the objects in my father's art collection, and the work that most delayed a banging gavel at the auction where I finally cleaned house, was nothing more galvanic than an unmarked sheet of paper with four pinholes in its corners.

This page was not just art but art of consequence, and the only thing that differentiated it from the bundled stacks you buy at Office Depot was an artist's uncorroborated claim that he had stared at it for a thousand hours.

Only in my earliest, most far-fetched daydreams had I ever been a cannibal the way that staring recluse was an artist, and I would never be someone who needed nothing but one hypnotizing spot upon a wall to make me happy, whether it contained a piece of paper being fired up by my eyesight or a peephole that could lull me into using my imagination as a lifeboat.

In that suspicious, coked-up moment with the missing boy's alleged image ringing in my eyes and the lawyer's phone call still engraved in my attention, I realized that, since I had never doodled anything that looked like much of anything, and since there were no secret passages around to stimulate my inner voyeur, I would be wise to reconsider acting.

Then I had a revelation, and not just any shocker but a bombshell that exploded the conclusion I had drawn about myself the night I synced a fading mental image of Alfonse beset with hungry lions to the riotous ejaculate I'd just nick-named Lake Stomach.

Barring my loft's lack of proscenium and rows of seats, and given that the sun or lamps in my vicinity weren't roving spotlights to my knowledge, I was and had been acting for as long as I could tell the difference.

When I spoke, I heard my father's voice, if not word for word then as loyally as the stars of Molière's plays had wagged his tongue in centuries.

If my life was even half the procedural unfolding of a game my father played, I'd barely coined a phrase outside the range of his remote control.

My brother, whom I'd only met at all because his father wore my mother's ring, was really more my understudy than a sibling, and Didier was less the makings of my boyfriend than Alfonse's stuntman.

What's that saying . . . if it resembles a duck and quacks, it's usually a duck? And if the world revolves around a duck, and experts claim it must since ducks see things and everyone, no matter their complexity or power, as basic shapes that are digestible or obstacle, then . . . well, I know I had a point when I began that.

Maybe I warrant your indulgence as I stared into my future on that scattered afternoon, reenvisioning my father as an artist who couldn't squint into a dent without creating a black hole, and Alfonse and I as sons who'd never masturbated without gluing down a piece of his collage, and the playhouse as a theater where I, the most anointed of his fantasies, could become the actor I'd been groomed to play.

Before I learned the marbled swarm, or, rather, spoiled its chances with my inattentiveness and patchy wit, then screwed up both of my impending lives, I believed I was my family's chief ingredient, if not for any evidence more solid than my highly complimented looks, then with total confidence.

Perhaps because it felt so unfamiliar at the time, there came a night when I was memorably alone and isolated, even though my family was in easy walking distance.

My mother had just burnt some corner of our dinner, locked the door, and was sulking on the kitchen floor as if it were a bathroom.

Alfonse was in his bedroom playing Go with an imaginary friend who, considering his mazy name was later solved into an anagram of mine, was probably a more perfected me.

My father, who consistently ignored me, was doing so while obfuscated by the mansion's secret tunnels, meaning somewhere so unknown I couldn't make-believe his negligence had been mandated by my rallying effect upon his every thought.

I was in the living room, for reasons no more interesting than the reason it was called a living room, worrying that, were my heart one of those malformed hand grenade–like hearts that crumple strapping soccer players in their twenties, my corpse might lie decomposing on the floor for hours.

I was sitting on a hexagonal clump of painted wood that met my father's standards for a couch, weakened by self-pity, yes, but more importantly because that clump was close to our TV.

If you wonder why I've paused to re-create this slight occasion when, up until this point, I've scrapped each time I'd qualified for couch potato or used the toilet, just be glad I care enough to skip you past the moiré pattern that diffused the TV screen and my attention for almost an hour thanks to my corresponding pickiness.

Instead, I'll strand us on a channel in the upper hundreds. It was showing an older film, not so old it lied the world was black and white, but too slushy-looking to have been fed through a computer, and too raggedy to have its origins in France, but dubbed into a slangy French, and thus something a thirteen-year-old boy like me could fancy were he stoned or strange enough.

Perhaps it was an actor whose famous name escapes me that stalled my finger on the button, but it was someone younger clad in nothing but an open, flapping medieval bathrobe and shoving human meat into his mouth who made me stop.

It was an avant-garde film, as they were called, so, where a film you'd actually choose to watch would have a story line, it had jagged cuts from place to place and interminable close-ups of the human soul tinkering with actors' eyes. Still, as I'd seen my mother act in even weirder pictures, I sort of figured out the deal behind the character I seemed to like.

He'd killed his father, fled into a forest, and was hunting guys and eating them because, well, snakes and lizards must taste as scary as they look.

Since I didn't know a cannibal from Tintin at that point, my first reactions weren't "how gross" or "that's so fucking awesome," but rather broodings of the wistful, wanton sort particular to thirteen-year-old inverts like myself who thought the parts of life that didn't give me an erection weren't especially important.

So intensely good-looking was this cannibal, and so greatly did the actor's face improve on every face for which I now felt I'd made considerable allowances, that I wondered if I'd even seen this film before, perhaps when still so tiny and half blind I thought his image was a lesson on my babysitters' flash cards.

I tend to watch the films I rent or download with the rashness of a porn fan whose arousal is dependent on one offbeat speck of sex, say nipple play, and yet I found the hour while this film unspooled in arty, traipsing increments no problem whatsoever.

Even when the cannibal was captured by an antiquated version of police, then kept from eating as he liked or skinny-dipping as I wished, I endured that quarrelsome couch in hopes the actor's name might brake the closing credits lengthily enough that I could run upstairs and Google him.

If you think I'm complicated as it stands, feel fortunate I lack the courage to delineate my mind's implosion when the scroll of names revealed him as Pierre Clémenti and the body I had craved to be essentially my own with just a few years' muscle tone to separate us.

While I won't lie that I've been secretly dictating what you're reading from a wheelchair, having long since gnawed away my limbs like a coyote in a snare trap, I will reveal that, among the details I've withheld to spare us my embarrassment are a large number of mirrors that I feel my living quarters would be dull without.

If you've wished this story had included an additional sex scene or a hundred, or if you think that, for all the many paintings made to illustrate the story of Narcissus swooning at a pond, there remains the urgent need for an XXX-rated version starring me, well, I agree with you objectively, but no.

Point is, I'd just longed to fuck my father then, presumably, be killed by him and eaten, or, given our resemblance, vice versa, or, in other words, to somehow eat myself without committing suicide, and that was quite a shock, no question there, but it was more the kind of shock I'd felt when the chateau I purchased early in our friendship showed itself as yet another batch of secret tunnels masquerading as a home. In other words, it was the pattern of my self-regard that petrified me.

I must have sat there glazing in the film's postscript of clustered advertisements while my thoughts turned uglier and uglier for quite a while, I don't remember.

Eventually, the room was acclimated by the odor of our salvaged dinner. While I'm sure my mother's cooking did my stomach's trick, I do remember that the cow who'd died to set my teeth in motion seemed no more instrumental to the flavor than any fish who might have swum the Evian with which I washed it down.

No occasion in real life is as loaded as the scene in every film I can remember where some actor turns his cheerless eyes—or, rather, pulls a well-known acting trick that makes his eyes appear lamentable—upon his loved ones. Then, looking away, often out a window where a stretch of nature dominates and looks idyllic, his eyes will signal us that, when he kills himself or them, we, having watched that scene, will understand his reasons as completely or as poorly as he ever did.

It's a venerable device, and suggesting that my thoughts that night were pivotal is a device as well, but why not save us time and join me in believing it.

In the days, months, and gradually years since I decided to impersonate my real and less realistic father—although it's true that both of them had made their names by living lies—I've made do and even headway as a cannibal.

I've wolfed down sawed-off torsos like a zombie or Neanderthal, and I've applied ivory chopsticks and the most delicate of forks to nibbles that procrastinated in my mouth like soggy laundry in a drier. Still, let me put two names to two examples and, more important, finish off some stories that would dangle off a final cliff rather than closing sentence.

Serge, or #7 as we know him, was deducted in a surgical procedure that, although heavily modified by Christophe, was invented in the 1990s to salvage living sculptures from the husks of people who had set themselves on fire, for instance. We ate his highlights while, on a narrow, adjunct table, his rags blinked once for "thanks" and twice for "yes" when we voiced compliments or questions.

Claude, whom you'll recall as #7's brother, was discovered dead inside the clothes and makeup of his mother—the victim of a topple, we decided, although the dinner he supplied had a metallic taste that might have warranted a coroner had François not, on that occasion, cooked a feast that left so little of the boy behind—and, as I recall, he was down to fingernails and toenails—that we would have had more luck extracting DNA from his reflection in a window.

But now I'm speaking of and as the fussy, rock-hard brute that cast the palest shadow in my thirteen-year-old daydreams.

For reasons lost to whimsy's transience but logical in theory, I felt a need to ditch my heedless family, not through moping in some fraction of our mansion but by reviving someone I had also been until perhaps a year before.

That younger, less envisioned me would sneak away from home some nights, then mosey through the park that partners with the Eiffel Tower—i.e., a numbing stretch of lawn and chintzy trees that seemed less conjured from the ground than sanded free of buildings like the land around an airport.

It seemed a kind of giant, threadbare cushion where, were the Eiffel Tower to be wrenched from its foundations by some angry King Kong type, it could land without untoward expense. In the meantime, tourists were free to come and go.

At the age of eight or nine, I'd used these walkabouts to blend into the people milled beneath the Tower whence, adopting some cartoony foreign accent and uncovering my fractured English, I would ask a fellow novice for directions to some tourist trap. Normally, one or two successful scams would undermine my loneliness and turn me on my heel.

But when my voice stockpiled its current rust, my loss for words and phony accents seemed to work against me. No matter how unfashionably I dressed or spoke, every tourist I intrigued would winnow Paris from our chats until we only seemed to speak about the view from his hotel room, wherein the Louvre or Notre Dame was inevitably visible.

In far too many cases, I was persuaded that I wouldn't have seen Paris until I saw it through their window, and, once I had, feel equally convinced that, since Paris was a state of mind, I might know it best when least distracted by its details, courtesy, they suggested, of a close-up of a pillow I would spend an hour biting and deluging with my tears and slobber.

On the evening I'm beginning to describe, it was this willful ignorance of Paris I found touristic.

My strolling and sightseeing quickly centered on two boys a little older than myself—Swedish, I thought, or from those other, nearby states that crank out blonds and seem like lesser

Swedens—whose faces wore the stares I always leave in faces once I've shown them any interest.

To steal away with foreigners who don't speak French or who flip through phrase books while they're bantering, I must retrain my mouth to gum the basic, neutralizing English that all Europeans speak when taking breaks outside their homelands.

In other words, you wouldn't recognize me, but, on the plus side, you could feel the full, calamitous effect of my infamously hot, false first impression.

Just as hosts will use the minutes prior to guests' arrival tidying the messes in their homes that seem too fine to whitewash in their normal course of vacuuming, I spent the cab ride to the Swedes' hotel scoping out my body language to make sure I'd left myself back at the mansion.

Their hotel was a filthy stack of floors between two crepe stands on rue St. André des Arts. As we climbed the stairs, they spoke of our responsibility to have ingenious sex while high above a street trodden by visionary poets and experimental writers whose names were granulated by their Swedish accents and adorned the messy pile of books that made their unmade double bed look like a table.

As I've mentioned, having sex is always new to me, and I am less its star than an inspector who assigns himself the case, and who is not so much assigned as stranded there, and every bed is like an open road, and I some clueless rabbit lingering in danger's path because it needs the warmth.

True to form or any lack thereof, when the Swedes offered to take my coat, they might as well have been a pair of blinding headlights. Stricken by my piddling English and a voice whose squeaks I can't affect in my loquacious current form, I tried to warn them that, although I'd been declared a lousy lay by everyone who'd had the job before them, if they truly were fans of miscreants like Baudelaire, perhaps they would find poetry where others had felt miserable.

I distantly recall the day when I mistyped onto a website where some boys around my age were busy milking one another's bodies of what seemed to be a magic potion that I only learned through trial and error was no better than the crummy snacks in mine.

Still, at that time, based on their swabbing tongues and chomping teeth and pawing hands, you might have thought the mouth or cock or ass they worked on was a secret passage and they would have tried to crawl inside had they not been relatively gigantic.

I've never misconstrued an ass or cock or mouth as bottomless, but mine have been exhausted like they were and more routinely than I've cared to say, and being fucked is not what I imagined, and, in fact, I'll ask for your indulgence if I edit my involvement to a look of terror that, on second thought, I might not dwell on either since the Swedes were far more interested in shoving things inside my face than understanding me with its help.

That lasted long enough that I began to think—well, as much as someone trying not to cry can think, and maybe it's the terms "intuit" or "feel" I should be grasping for—that, when I'd let my acting teacher fool around to get the role of Chevalier Danceny in *Les liaisons dangereuses*, then padded my few lines so loosely he was fired as an incompetent, the central problem might have been when he'd miscast me as the sexiest kid he'd ever seen, I think he said.

But, since you weren't in bed with us, let me try a populist example, although I will admit in doing so that I'm just parroting what others far more well informed have written.

Apparently, there is a novel titled *Story of the Eye* that, although mistaken by French readers in the '50s for porn just erudite enough to carry on the metro, was instead a work of genius that co-opted the erotic—a kind of sheep in wolf's clothing—and this novel's eminence is such that it was prominent among the volumes lying open on the Swedes' bed and the second to the last to be knocked onto the floor.

Its success led hornier authors with fewer ulterior designs to dress their novels' sexy scenes in Linguist Chic. The most famous of these knockoffs is *The Story of O*. It and novels titled virtually like it seemed to titillate a marginally better class of reader on release, but their steamy scenes were too uncomplicated for the French intelligentsia and their artfulness too thin to work as a deodorant.

Nowadays, these books are only valued for their frilly raunch by boys too nice to hack the monitoring software off their pantywaist computers, and when the books are spoken of with multisyllables, it usually involves a backward compliment about their porn's off-putting gussiness, which certain brainiacs find interestingly camp.

Obviously, when I discuss these shallow novels, it's a roundabout self-portrait, and when I parse their readership, I speak obliquely of the Swedes as well as every ex for whom I've seemed to guarantee an orgasm so rash they might have gotten pregnant through their hands had I not been there to swallow it.

These invading and intersecting thoughts or insecurities or revisions or what have you, and how they gnarl and loop my thinking, and how that coarsens my appearance, and how this worries me, are what I have instead of sex when guys are having sex with how I look, and that's all I have to show you in return, which is largely why I haven't.

This is why I crawl in beds mythologized, and why I'm forcibly removed from them, then slump in taxis crumpling paper scraps not scribbled with new boyfriends' numbers and addresses but inscribed with book titles like *Outliving Your*

Depression or referrals to their friends who also happen to be psychiatrists.

So, once the Swedes had fucked and eaten out and squatted on my face until its ornaments were worn away and my responses seemed as automated as a cuckoo clock's . . . when the standard English praise I had elicited gave way to Swedish terms I didn't understand and which they shouted so consistently it almost seemed like they were beating me to death . . . once the expression in my eyes lost its parenthetical mystique and started giving updates on the current level of my general agreement . . . once I wasn't worth the extra effort to distinguish from the other sluts and bitches they'd called sluts and bitches . . . when I was just the hands and knees on which a quote-unquote tight ass was placed at a convenient height and, to hear them, thanks to them . . . when they closed their eyes and started snoring more than breathing, and caromed off me like sleepwalkers who were bumping into walls . . .

Suddenly, their bed was mine, and I was someone they'd seen freaking out beneath the Eiffel Tower and safeguarded home out of guilt or decency. When my tears and howls were willing, I could barely see them, hastily half dressed, glassy-eyed, and nodding to the violent rhythm of my outburst.

What I confessed, to no avail since, between their erstwhile grasp of English and the tyrannical French accent that scrawls my erstwhile grasp of English, I might as well have been a suicide bomber using beatbox vocal tricks to imitate the sound of an explosion, was the horrifyingly uncomplicated truth.

It was a truth so honest and completely unironic that even I, who presumably believed myself, didn't understand its point, or why this authenticity had shown up now when I felt least in need of rescuing, or how it wound up in my mouth, or why my mouth was such a bullhorn, or where it had been hiding from the words I'd always used to talk my way around it.

I've failed the marbled swarm as I semi-understand its rules and premise, and, although you'll never know the difference, barring errors that weren't meant as an insidious direction, there is nowhere deeper or more intricately stifled by my story than this hotel room, and I'm out of means to keep you waiting for the secret that involved my sleight of hand unless you think a very frightened thirteen-year-old boy who looks vaguely like Pierre Clémenti seems magical or promising enough.

Acknowledgments

Dennis Cooper is very grateful to Yury Smirnov, Gisele Vienne, Joel Westendorf, Ira Silverberg, Michael Signorelli, Carrie Kania, Justin Dodd, Paul Otachovsky-Laurens, Emmelene Landon, Catherine Robbe-Grillet, and Chrystel Dozias.

BOOKS BY DENNIS COOPER

UGLY MAN
Stories

ISBN 978-0-06-171544-0 (paperback)

"Cooper's writing in *Ugly Man* is like a highly literate game of hot-hands—you never know when he's going to hit you next, but by the time it's all over you feel that distinctive stinging sensation."

—*LA Weekly*

SMOTHERED IN HUGS
Essays, Interviews, Feedback, and Obituaries

ISBN 978-0-06-171561-7 (paperback)

"Cooper delivers with the unswerving faith of someone who lives and dies by his gut reactions but also with the methodical intelligence of someone who parses those reactions so he can articulate them to the sharpest degree."

—*Los Angeles Times*